MW01138488

ADVANCED

POTION

MAKING

Advanced Potion Making
Second Edition

Copyright © 2004 by Mythos Books
Printed and Bound by Mythos Books

ISBN: 978-1-312-94792-4

All quotations, unless otherwise indicated, are taken from
ADVANCED POTION MAKING First Edition, Copyright
© 2015 by Mythos Books

Glossary

Introduction

The potions within this book are considered advanced in as much as each of them is not only difficult to produce, but also contain the possibility of being disastrous if done incorrectly. Students should only attempt potions herein under the supervision and tutelage of a Potion Master.

Nomenclature in advanced potion making — as an art and not simply as the title of this work — can be quite confusing due to the fact the chemical names often bear no relation to composition. For example, lead sulfide is sometimes referred to as the "black sulfur root" because of its colour and the heat used in its preparation from sulfur. While the authors of this book have taken every measure to insure use of only the most common nomenclatures mistakes should be avoided by cross referencing the symbol chart as much as possible; students may also wish to keep personal notes and annotations in a separate notebook.

It is advisable for students to take careful note of processes as outlined within; Distillation, Coagulation, Dissolution, Filtration, Calcination, Deconstruction, and Reconstruction; Infusion, Crushing, Cutting, Boiling, Scalding and Straining. Each of these processes are unique in effect and students should not interchange them without the express guidance of a Potion Master.

A note on alchemy
as proto-magic

A common misperception of ancient alchemists was that they were pseudo wizards who attempted to turn lead into gold, create love from concoction alone, and believed that the universe was composed of only the four elements of earth, air, fire, and water.

This picture was, obviously, rather unfair. Although some ancient alchemists were indeed crackpots and charlatans, most were well-meaning and intelligent wizards. These people in many ways served as innovators, and attempted to explore and investigate the nature of chemical substances and processes. They had to rely on experimentation, traditional know-how, rules of thumb — and speculative thought in their attempts to uncover the mysteries of the magical universe.

At the same time, it was clear to the alchemists that "something" was generally being conserved in chemical processes, even in the most dramatic changes of physical state and appearance; i.e. that substances contained some "principles" that could be hidden under many outer forms, and revealed by proper manipulation. Throughout the history of the discipline, alchemists struggled to understand the nature of these principles, and find some order and sense in the results of their experiments — which were often undermined by impure or poorly characterized reagents, the lack of quantitative measurements, and confusing and inconsistent nomenclature.

Alchemy and astrology

Since its earliest times, alchemy has been closely connected to astrology — which, in the Islamic world and Europe, generally meant the traditional Babylonian-Greek school of astrology. Alchemical systems often postulated that each of the seven planets known to the ancients "ruled" or was associated with a certain metal. See the separate article on astrology and alchemy for further details. In Hermeticism it is linked with both astrology and theurgy. "Everything that happens once will never happen again. But anything that happens twice will surely happen a third time." A quote from The Alchemist.

Relationship between wizard and potion

While the use of wands, incantations, and general skill are all relevant in general education and learning potion making they are even more so herein. Students should be mindful of their own abilities and should not attempt recipes they do not feel equipped to handle. It should be said that this is not a short coming and that the greatest potion masters in history have all had potions they will not attempt.

This book does not, therefore, contain any potions which would allow the student to build up a false sense of self thereby opening the gateway to greater peril in later studies. The book begins with a chapter on "Nearly Impossible Potions" and continues thusly.

Students unable to complete all the potions in this book should not be discouraged. A mastery in potions is a necessity for many careers in the magical world and students seeking magical government occupations should set their mind to accomplishing as much as magically possible.

A final thought from the publishers

Potions are tools just like spells. Keep your cauldron as close as your wand; in mind and heart if not in reality. With study, determination and a little hard work you can learn to entrance the mind and befuddle the senses. A true potion master can bottle acclaim, brew friendship, and even put a cork in suffering. If that doesn't excite you, you may have the wrong book.

Good luck!

Nearly Impossible
Potions

🖝 LOVE POTION

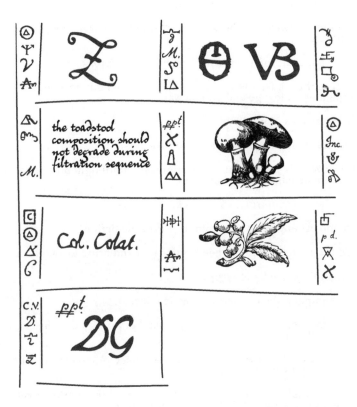

Recognizable by its distinctive luminescent sheen and by the fact that its steam rises in characteristic waves. The Love Potion smells differently to different people according to what attracts them. Though it's named the "love potion" it does not, in fact, really cause the person who drinks it to fall in love but instead to develop a powerful infatuation or obsession with the target.

The duration of the effects of the Love Potion vary depending on such factors as the weight of the person drinking the potion and the general attractiveness of the target — which is subjective.

☞ Instructions

1) Boil 1 bottle of red clotted milk wax for about 10 minutes in a silver cauldron until it's reduced by half.

2) Add the following and brew for at least 12 hours from the point of bubbling.

3) Allow the cauldron to return to room temperature.

4) Discard the toadstools and strain the riverweed out, reserving the serpent eggs, lovage and gnome wax.

5) Heat 2 scoops of goblin oil.

6) Add the toadstools back with 3 red rose petals

7) Brew over low heat for about 15 minutes or until light blue sparks are seen on the edges of the cauldron.

8) Transfer the cauldron to a steam bath.

9) Syphon off any excess oil from the top of the potion.

10) Add 1/2 goblet of acrobat beetle juice to it and bring to a boil.

11) Boil until reduced and syrupy.

12) Add another goblet of acrobat beetle juice.

13) Bring to a boil, scraping away any crust that forms along the edges and reduces the sparking.

14) Cover the cauldron with a wet, wrinkled sheet of parchment paper and then a tight fitting lid.

15) Brew on weak fire for 4 hours 37 minutes, until the sparks subside and the potion has a pearl-like sheen to its surface.

16) Gather 13 large daisy petals and toast them individually over an open flame evenly on both sides.

- **They should be lightly browned with no black edges.**

17) In a mortar pound or grind the petals along with another goblet of diced lovage into a thick paste.

18) Discard the paper and add the lovage/daisy petal paste.

19) Using a levitation incantation, transfer the target's personal item (hair, bit of clothing, etc.) to the cauldron.

  - **It should be noted that the target's personal item should never be touched by anyone but the target.**

  - **A burst of smoke should appear the moment the target's personal item is completely submerged and continue to slowly rise in a spiral manner.**

20) Your potion preparation is now complete.

Serve as a draught, or use in baking or other confectioneries; further heat, cooking or addition to items which are altered here out will not disrupt the potion. Best served in wine.

Esprits acides.
Acide du sel marin.
Acide nitreux.
Acide vitriolique.
Sel alcali fixe.
Sel alcali volatil.

Terre absorbante.
Substances metalliques.
Mercure.
Regule d'Antimoine.
Or.
Argent.

☞ Substitutions

Goblin oil can be substituted with certain gnome oils which have been prepared specifically for Love Potion. Ask your local apothecary or potions master for help when procuring them.

Silver coated pewter cauldrons are acceptable and will work. It should be noted, however, that they have often been found to cause a weaker or shorter lasting Love Potion.

Rose petals may be used in place of daisy petals. In this case they should be toasted on only one side and only until the perfume of the petal is released. Rose petals cause more of a "dream like" state in the patient and has been known to cause the potion to be somewhat harder to control the target.

☞ Notes

If the smoke burst appears at any point before the target's personal item is submerged destroy the potion and cauldron immediately.

Students should keep a close eye on their cauldron during the entire two-day brewing process as it is possible, however unlikely, that rancid goblin oil can cause certain undesirable effects. Signs of these effects beginning are light refracting smoke, green (not blue) sparks appearing around the edges of the cauldron, or a severe reduction and/or expansion of the potion between stages 3 and 4. If any of these are noted alert your potions master at once.

Familiars should not inhale or digest this potion neither after completion nor during any part of the process past stage I.

Use on oneself is severely discouraged.

☞ DRINK OF WAKING DEATH

$AsCl_3 + 3KJ \rightarrow$ $AsJ_3 + 3KCl$ $Be + Cl_2 \rightarrow$ $BeCl_2$		$CaCO_3 + heat \rightarrow$ $CaO + CO_2.$ Inc.		
Twenty Degrees of				
Ninth Degree				
$HCO + H \rightarrow$ H_2CO (rate constant = $9.2 \times 10^{-3} s-1$)		Twenty Degrees of		
Z		In the Hour of		
Eighteenth Degrees of				

The Drink of Waking Death is an extremely powerful sleeping potion. It sends the drinker into a deep trance that mimics the state of death. The potion should resemble a smooth, black melted wax liquid at the halfway stage; it should then turn a light shade of turquoise, then almost invisible when completed.

◼☞ Instructions

1) Begin by making certain the cauldron is completely clean of any dust and debris.

2) Add 500 ml of stagnant water until bubbling slowly.

3) Add the in 4 of the 20 valerian roots, one at each key point of the cauldron circle.

- **Take no more than 30 seconds to do this task.**

4) Divide the sloth brain into quarters.

5) Add one quarter of the sloth brain to cauldron.

- **Be mindful to not allow cauldron to boil over.**

6) Stir the cauldron for 5 minutes, clockwise, at a whisking pace.

7) Rotate the cauldron counterclockwise on the flame 45°.

8) Add in 6 more of the 20 valerian roots, one at each complimentary point of the cauldron circle.

9) Carefully cut the sopophorous bean in two and extract as much juice as possible.

10) Add 7 drops of the wormwood from one of each of the viles. Make sure there are no drips on the edges of the cauldron.

11) Stir the potion 10 times clockwise.

- **Your potion now should be resembling black melted wax.**

13) Slowly pour 7 square pieces of asphodel petals & stir the potion 10 times anti-clockwise.

14) Add 150 oz. of powered Dragon Horn.

15) Your potion preparation is now complete.

⅊ Zinc
PC Pierre Calaminaire.

Θ SeL
Ѵ Esprit de vin et Esprit ar

[dents

☞ Substitution

No substitutions are allowed.

☞ Notes

While brewing, the potion releases blue steam. The ideal halfway stage should be of a black colour (deep purple), although at a later stage if stirred properly the potion will turn a light shade of turquoise and then, eventually, "almost invisible."

Testing the effectiveness of the potion is easily done with the leaf or petal of any flowering plant. Simply dip the plant half way into the potion and withdraw it. The dipped section will disintegrate as if being burned. No ash, however, nor any other signs of item will remain but only the area untouched with a very clean line where it was submerged.

If any residue is left of any kind the potion is a failure and should be discarded.

☠ *Caput Mortuum* 3ſ,ƀ ⚗

$Cl-$ (181.4), $Br-$ (4.2), $SO_{4}2-$ (0.4), $HCO_{3}-$ (0.2), $Ca_{2}+$ (14.1), $Na+$ (32.5), $K+$ (6.2) and $Mg_{2}+$ (35.2)

☞ PEACE GIVER

The Peace Giver is a potion which relieves anxiety and agitation. Its ingredients are powdered pumice stone, powdered troll ears, and powdered pegasus hooves. It should be a turquoise blue when finished and simmered before being drunk.

This draught is ironically difficult and making a mistake can have drastic consequences. Adding too much of the ingredients, for instance, will put the drinker of the potion into a deep — and possibly irreversible — sleep.

Ingredients must be added exactly in order and amounts specified, and the potion needs to be stirred 7 times, both clockwise and anti-clockwise. Before the addition of the final ingredient, troll ears, the temperature of the flames must be lowered, and the potion allowed to simmer for seven minutes.

If brewed correctly, the potion will emit a lightly humming smoke, but the possible characteristics of a failed batch seem to be endless.

☞ Instructions

1) Add powdered pumice stone to 400 ml of basic potion starter until the potion turns green.

2) Stir until the potion turns blue.

3) Add powdered pumice stone until the potion turns purple.

4) Allow to simmer until the potion turns pink.

5) Add liquid until the potion turns turquoise.

   • **Do not add with high flame.**

6) Allow to simmer until the potion turns purple.

7) Shake powdered powdered troll ears vigorously until well separated and then sprinkle in until the potion turns red.

   • **Keep at constant temp as quills are added.**

8) Stir until the potion turns orange.

9) Add more powdered troll ears until the potion turns turquoise.

10) Allow to simmer till the potion turns purple.

11) Add powdered pegasus hooves until the potion turns pink.

12) Stir until the potion turns red.

13) Allow to simmer until the potion turns purple.

14) Add more powdered pumice stone until the potion turns grey.

15) Allow the potion to simmer until it turns orange.

16) Add more powdered powdered troll ears until the potion turns white.

☞ Substitution

No substitutions are allowed.

☞ Notes

Stop potion and discard if any of the following occur: green sparks, dark grey steam, a sulfurous odour, or a cement-like consistency.

☞ OLD AGE POTION

An Old Age Potion is a potion which causes the drinker to become older to a degree which is measurable by other sciences. The more of the potion is drunk, the larger the aging which occurs.

The effects of this potion are to be temporary and usually last anywhere from 8 to 12 hours.

Luna has from Venus, with Gemini and Libra, its measure of coagulation and its From Saturn, with Virgo and Scorpio, its homogeneous body, with gravity. From Sol, with Leo and Virgo, its spotless purity and great constancy against the power of fire. Such is the knowledge of the natural exaltation and of the course of the spirit and body of Luna, with its composite nature and wisdom briefly summarised.

☞ Instructions

1) Heat 450 ml of full-moon oil over medium heat in copper cauldron.

2) Add balmony by syphoning in through glass flask.

3) Simmer until the balmony is smoking, about 12 minutes.

4) Potion will begin to burn; as it burns repeat incantation 3 times.

5) Wave your wand.

6) Add in half of a scorched maiden hair fern.

7) Grind the wormwood in pestle until paste-like consistency is reached.

8) Add paste-like wormwood while waving wand clockwise.

9) Rub an image of the subject with cinquefoil and add image to potion.

10) Let boil 37 seconds.

11) Cover and let rest 45 minutes.

12) Remove from fire and allow to cool.

☞ Substitution

A personal item may be substituted for an image in Steps 9 & 10. The item should be something that is known by all to belong to the subject.

☞ Notes

The mixture you created should go bubbly and taste like a bitter-lemonade. The bubbles that form when you add the baking soda to the lemon mixture are carbon dioxide (CO_2), these are the same bubbles you'll find in proper fizzy drinks. Of course they add a few other flavored sweeteners but it's not much different to what you made. If you are wondering how the carbon dioxide bubbles formed, it was because you created a chemical reaction when you added the lemon (an acid) to the baking soda (a base).

The seventh canon.

Concerning the nature of Sol and its properties.

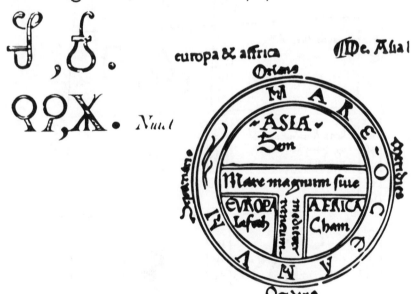

☛ BLACK FIRE POTION

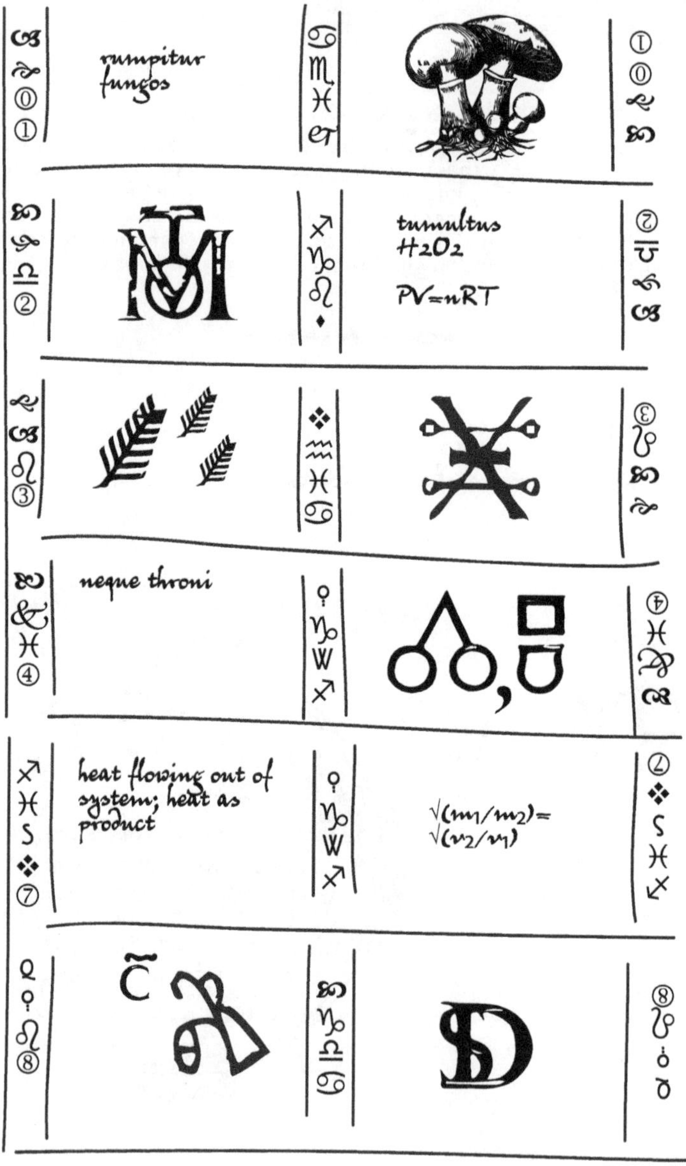
rumpitur fungos
tumultus
H2O2
PV=nRT
neque throni
heat flowing out of system; heat as product
√(m1/m2)=
√(v2/v1)

Fire Protection Potion, also known as Ice Potion, is a potion used to move through flames unscathed. When drunk, it induces a sensation of ice and frigidity in the drinker, and provides protection from most magical fires.

But for Sol, when the heat is withdrawn and the cold supervenes after liquefaction, to coagulate and to become hard and solid, there is need of the other five metals, whose nature it embraces in itself – Jupiter, Saturn, Mars, Venus, Luna. In these five metals the cold abodes with their regimens are especially found. Hence it happens that Sol can with difficulty be liquefied without the heat of fire, on account of the cold whereof mention has been made. For Mercury cannot assist with his natural heat or liquefaction, or defend himself against the cold of the five metals, because the heat of Mercury is not sufficient to retain Sol in a state of liquefaction. Wherefore Sol has to obey the five metals rather than Mercury alone. Mercury itself has no office of itself save always to flow. Hence it happens that in coagulations of the other metals it can effect nothing, since its nature is not to make anything hard or solid, but liquid. To render fluid is the nature of heat and life, but cold has the nature of hardness, consolidation, and immobility, which is compared to death.

The six cold metals, Jupiter, Venus, Saturn, Mars, Venus, Luna, if they are to be liquefied must be brought to that condition by the heat of fire. Snow or ice, which are cold, will not produce this effect, but rather will harden. As soon as ever the metal liquefied by fire is removed therefrom, the cold, seizing upon it, renders it hard, congealed, and immovable of itself. But in order that Mercury may remain fluid and alive continually, say, I pray you, whether this will be affected with heat on cold? Whoever answers that this is brought about by a cold and damp nature, and that it has its life from cold – the promulgator of this opinion, having no knowledge of Nature, is led away by the vulgar. For the vulgar man judges only falsely, and always holds firmly on to his error. So then let him who loves truth withdraw therefrom. Mercury, in fact, lives not at all from cold but from a warm and fiery nature. Whatever lives is fire, because heat is life, but cold the occasion of death.

☞ Instructions

1) Heat a mixture of 30 ml liquified moss and 70 ml goat milk.

2) Slice bursting mushrooms with knife and add to cauldron one slice at a time — no more than 4 slices per mushroom.

3) Drain any excess mushroom juice from cutting surface into cauldron.

4) Stir clockwise 8 times clockwise.

   • **or until potion turns blue.**

5) Add 3 ounces of blue salamander blood to cauldron.

6) Brew potion for 5 hours on medium heat.

7) Stir anti-clockwise.

   • **until potion turns green.**

8) Crush wartcap in pestle until fine and powder begins to to clump onto sides of mortar.

9) Add wartcap powder to cauldron by tapping it out of the pestle and making sure it does not touch anything besides the mortar and pestle on the way into the cauldron.

10) Brew for 3 hours 16 minutes on low heat or until potion stops smoking.

11) Stir clockwise (approximately 15 times).

   • **until potion turns red.**

12) Wave wand and your potion is complete.

☞ Substitution

Rotten mushrooms may be used in Step 1 in place of bursting mushrooms, however, potency should be tested if substitution is made.

☛ FORGETFULNESS POTION - ADVANCED

The Forgetfulness Potion causes an unknown degree of memory loss in the drinker. The degree of memory loss is equal to the amount of the potion consumed and the strength of the potion but is "unknown" because it is unmeasurable. It is roughly estimated that the amount of memory loss is approximately one hour of directed time to one swallow of normal strength Forgetfulness Potion.

This version of the Forgetfulness Potion is considered more advanced and is not the same as that listed in "Magical Drafts" as one is able to control which memories are to be forgotten. Memory loss is not permanent and subjects will fully regain their memories approximately 24 to 78 hours after ingesting it.

☞ Instructions

1) Add 2 drops of Lethe river water to your cauldron.

2) Gently heat for 20 seconds.

3) Add 2 Valerian sprigs to your cauldron.

4) Stir 3 times, clockwise.

5) Wave your wand.

6) Leave to brew and return in 45-60 minutes.

7) Create an enchanted paper with a detailed description of the memory you wish the subject to forget by holding the paper above the potion smoke as you write. The more specific the better but generalities work just as well.

8) Drop the paper into the cauldron.

9) Add 2 measures of standard ingredient to the mortar.

10) Add 4 mistletoe berries to the mortar.

11) Crush into a medium-fine powder using the pestle.

12) Add 2 pinches of the crushed mixture to your cauldron.

13) Stir 5 times, anti-clockwise.

14) Wave your wand to complete the potion.

Safran de Mars

Mendacem memorem esse oportet.
Memento mori.

Cogitationes posteriores sunt saniores.

☞ SERVUS VELLE

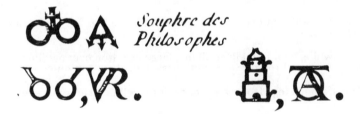

$$P_1 + P_2 + P_3 \ldots = P \text{ (total)}$$

PM=ƆRT

Souphre des Philosophes

$w = -P\Delta V$; positive when being done on the system; negative when being done by the system

The Servus Velle concoction will temporarily enslave the subject to the maker's will. The subject will have no memory of what was done during the time of effect though most often is aware that time is "missing." The subject will obey any command even if if it personally life threatening.

The subject also may exhibit increase in strength, agility, and healing during the time when they're under the effects of the potion.

☞ Instructions

1) Heat cauldron to medium heat.

2) Add 25 ml liver oil.

3) Season toad legs with moonseed and nightshade.

4) Cook toad legs in batches until browned, 5-6 minutes per side. Transfer to a plate.

5) Add horned slug to cauldron; cook until rendered.

6) Add mandrake roots, riverweed stalks, and flabbergasted slug.

7) Cook until slug is translucent, 7-8 minutes.

8) Stir in 250 ml pond slime and lobalug venom paste.

9) Simmer for 2-3 minutes. Add remaining 750 ml pond slime.

10) Boil until pond slime is reduced by half, 15-20 minutes.

11) Return toad legs to cauldron.

12) Add syrup of arnica.

13) Tie thyme and rosemary sprigs together; add to cauldron.

14) Bring to a boil and cover.

15) Transfer cauldron to oven and braise until toad legs are tender, about 1 1/4 hours.

16) Meanwhile, heat 14 ml liver oil in a large cauldron over medium-high heat. Add mushrooms; sauté until browned, about 5 minutes.

17) Transfer toad legs from sauce to cauldron with mushrooms; keep warm.

18) Simmer sauce over medium heat until reduced by 1/3, about 20 minutes.

19) Season with moonseed and nightshade.

☞ Notes

Most often recognized in Voodoo witchcraft as the "zombie maker."

☞ CANIS ORATIO

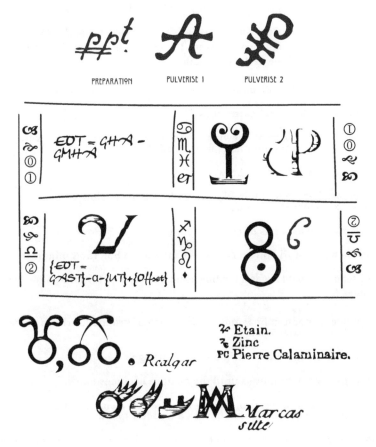

PREPARATION   PULVERISE 1   PULVERISE 2

Etain.
Zinc
PC Pierre Calaminaire.

Realgar

Marcas
suie

The Canis Oratio potion will give any relatively intelligent canine the ability to speak. The animal will only be able to speek a language it knows — i.e. a language it has been exposed to. Wild dogs, for example, may only speak in a different animal language rendering the effects of the potion nill.

▣☞ Instructions

1) Pluck a few hairs from the back of an unwashed canine's skull.

   • **to find the best location simply put one finger on each ear of the dog and move them to the middle of the head. Then trace the line back towards the tail until you find the back of the skull.**

2) Heat 250 ml of basic potion starter in a standard sized cauldron.

3) Add canine hairs to heated brew.

4) Bite off one square of chewing tobacco and gently chew gently for approximately one minute (spit as needed).

5) Add chewed tobacco to brew.

6) Increase heat to medium high and allow to begin slow boil for approximately 30 minutes.

7) Add two tablespoons of coffee grounds.

8) Raise heat to full boil and allow the mixture to boil for 5 minutes.

   • **the tobacco should act as a binding agent and begin to turn the potion light golden brown.**

9) Reduce to medium heat and mix in a dash of ground fabricata and a pinch of speekleweed.

10) Wait for the mixture to turn a radiant orange.

11) Stir gently for 2 minutes until the mixture becomes black.

12) Using a fine strainer transfer the mixture into a small cauldron pushing any excess liquid out with a wooden spoon.

   • **the liquid will be black like watery ink not jet black like ink. If it is jet black like ink then you will need to add a drop of viscous matter from an eye of a teen Enn which will momentarily turn the liquid a very bright royal blue before settling into a nice "watery ink".**

13) In a mortar add a pinch of finely ground rosetta clay and two petals from the purple polkadotted dictionarius flower. Grind with pestle until a fine powder is produced.

14) Sprinkle powder ontop of the "inky" extractus.

☛ Notes

Once completed you may dehydrate as desired or bottle for a later date.

If dehydrated simply add a couple of pinches to some meat and feed to the subject - if the subject speech is slowed or slurred continue to put more pinches in more food for the subject. The subject may attempt to slow their speech so as to trick you into giving them more meat.

If the entire brew is bottled in liquid form then you may add up to one tablespoon to meat or place it in the water

The subject should retain speech for up to 90 minutes.

Placing the potion in the subject's water will dilute the mixture and the mixture will then build over time and increase the amount of time the subject will retain speech.

You may dose a subject with an initial meat-treat then adding the suspension to the water so the dog will continue to speak.

☞ INCREMENTA SAPIENTIAE

The Incrementa Sapientiae potion temporarily improves the wisdom of the one who imbibes it. This is not a "book" or even "street" smart sort of wisdom but a true Wisdom — capital "W".

"The only true wisdom is in knowing you know nothing." - Socrates

☞ Instructions

1)   Heat owl feathers to medium-high heat on open flame and hold temperature for 20 min.

2)   Remove the owl feathers from flame and immediately dust tops with finely cut wizard beard hair.

3)   In a standard pewter cauldron stir together the sweetened Hippogryph milk and dried Ōrāculum.

4)   Slowly drizzle mixture over owl feathers.

5)   Allow the feathers to cool completely at room temperature, then chill for at least 1 hour.

6)   Boil black root in 250 ml of pure water until water is completely black and thick.

7)   Fold in 3 turtle egg whites.

8)   Crumble dried rose petals into mixture.

9)   Whip into froth.

10)   Allow to simmer for 20 minutes on low heat.

11)   Add chilled feathers to brew.

12)   Bring to boil for 1 hour.

13)   Burn shredded pages of an old text book.

14)   Add ashes to cauldron.

15)   Cover, remove from heat and allow to rest for 3 days. When opened a faint bluish grey smoke should be hovering just below the lid and above the potion itself.

☞ Notes

Hold nose and close eyes while imbibing.

☞ FORTUNA LIQUID

P.,S̃.

Inc.

Fortuna secundum

♃ *Mercury, quicksilv.*

Trifolium ½

[Xe] 4f14 5d10 6s2

Two Hundred Twenty Degrees of

Zosimos of Panopolis

Age quod agis.

80

200.59 ± 0.02 u

Fortuna Liquid is a magical potion that makes the drinker lucky for a period of time, during which everything they attempt will be successful.

It is meant to be used sparingly, however, as it causes giddiness, recklessness, and dangerous overconfidence if taken in excess. Fortuna Liquid is highly toxic in large quantities and is also a banned substance in all organised competitions along with all other methods of cheating. It is very difficult to make, disastrous if made wrong, and requires six months to brew before it is ready to be consumed.

☞ Instructions

1)   Add 2 drops of Lethe river water to your cauldron.

2)   Gently heat for 20 seconds.

3)   Add 2 Valerian sprigs to your cauldron.

4)   Stir 3 times, clockwise.

5)   Wave your wand.

6)   Leave to brew and return in 45-60 minutes.

7)   Create an enchanted object with a detailed wish imprint of good fortune. The imprints should not be specific but should instead be simply general good fortune as specific imprints of ideas, goals or desires tend to muddy the potion's effect. Allow the object to change your wishes as it is being imprinted if it so desires as this will actually lend itself to being a more suitable enchantment .

| GRADES OF FIRE | IMBIBITION | INCOMPLETE I | LUTATION SEALING I | LUTATION SEALING 2 | MIX | PER DELIQUIUM |

8)   Drop the enchanted object into the cauldron.

9)   Add 2 measures of standard ingredient to the mortar.

10) Add 4 mistletoe berries to the mortar.

11) Crush into a medium-fine powder using the pestle.

12) Add 2 pinches of the crushed mixture to your cauldron.

13) Stir 5 times, anti-clockwise.

14) Allow to simmer, completely undisturbed, on a low fire for six full months. The timing must be six months exactly — to the hour, minute and preferably second. Once the time has expired remove from heat.

15) Wave your wand to complete the potion.

☞ Notes

Many believe that Fortuna Liquid does not actually make one "lucky" — as "luck", while very real and usable by magical creatures such as Leprechauns, is not a replicable magical property — but instead causes the subject to have a heightened sense of awareness of probability and understanding of relational theory. It also releases personal inhibitions and self-awareness which often hinders one who is trying to accomplish something. It is said that these two forces combine and cause one to simply become unable to fail - hence "lucky."

⚥, ⊕. *Fleur d'Antimoine*   ☷, ♄. *Laut réent*

♄, ♄. *Fleur de Saturne*   ♌, ♄. *Lampe*

Audaces fortuna iuvat – Audentes fortuna juvat.

Citius venit malum quam revertitur.

ADVANCED POTION MAKING

☞ MODO PLUS INCANTATORES

Row 1:
$E = h*$, where
$h = Planc's$
constant $= 6.62*1$

Row 2:
dissolute

Row 3:
$A_{x4}E$;
bond angle $90°$,
$120°$

Row 5:
A_{x3};
bond angle $120°$

$\Delta G° = \Sigma \Delta G°$
(products) $- \Sigma \Delta G°$
(reactants); Δ
$G° = RT(lnK)$; Δ
$G° = -nFE°$

Row 6:
totam
rem

Modo Plus Incantatores greatly increases and clarifies the drinker's sense of smell. The person taking this potion should easily be able to identify specific smells from over 3 miles away — depending on wind direction.

☞ Instructions

1) Dust your work area with powdered porcupine quill. Place the boom berries and the water in a large cauldron. Boil hard for 5 minutes until the berries are puffy and expanded.

2) Using your wand stir the berries until they are soft and smooth. If some berry pieces remain, return to the heat for 3-4 minutes, until the berry mixture is entirely smooth and free of lumps.

3) Add the powdered porcupine quill and begin to stir with wand. Stir until the quill begins to incorporate and it becomes impossible to stir anymore.

4) Scrape the berry-quill mixture out onto the prepared work surface. It will be sticky and lumpy, with lots of quill that has not been incorporated yet--this is normal. Dust your hands with powdered porcupine quill, and begin to knead the mixture like bread dough, working the quill into the berry mix with your hands.

5) Continue to knead the concoction until it smoothes out and loses its stickiness. Add more quill if necessary, but stop adding quill once it is smooth--too much quill will make it stiff and difficult to work with. Once the dough is a smooth ball, divide it evenly into three balls.

6) Take one of the dough balls and flatten it into a round disc. Add 4-5 drops of honey water to the centre of the disc, and fold the disc over on itself so that the honey water is enclosed in the centre of the dough ball.

7) Begin to knead the ball of dough just like you did before. As you work it, you will begin to see streaks of colour coming through from the centre. Continue to knead until the streaks are gone and the fondant is a uniform yellow colour. Repeat the process with the third small ball, adding the leech juice (or a combination of red and yellow to produce orange) so that you end up with three smooth dough balls, in white, yellow, and orange.

8) Now it is time to roll out the dough. If you have a very long workbench you can do it all at once, but if you are pressed for space you might find it easier to divide your dough balls in half and assemble the concoction in two batches.

9) On your powdered quill-coated workstation, begin to roll the yellow fondant ball into a long worm shape, using your palms to roll it into a very long, thin cylinder. The exact size will depend on your preference for the size of your finished concoction, recommended to keeping it around 2 cm thick. Try to keep it the same size along the length of the dough strip, but some minor variation is fine. Once the yellow worm is rolled out, repeat the process with the orange and the white strips, placing them next to each other when completed. When you finish you should have three long cylinders of yellow, orange, and white dough, each approximately the same length and width.

10) If your dough is slightly sticky, you should be able to press the strips together to create one unified dough strip with three colours. If they are well-dusted with powdered quill, they might not stick. If this is the case, you can wet a potion brush and lightly run it along the sides of the strips, and the water will cause them to fuse together.

11) Once your strips are firmly pressed together, you should be able to start cutting. Cutting them in their present state produces a rounded piece of dough. If you prefer, you can very gently run a rolling pin along the top of the tri-coloured dough strip, to flatten the tops and

press them closer together. Use a large, sharp knife to cut triangles out of the dough strip. The kernels will have alternating white and yellow tips.

12) Store in an airtight container at room temperature for several weeks. This concoction will get sticky if exposed to too much moisture, so it is best made and stored in a place with low humidity.

13) After storage time bake in a covered cauldron with a flat bottom for 30 min.

14) After 30 min pour in powdered fairy wing. Stir with wand until all kernels are coated.

15) Chill. Use 5 kernels at a time.

🖙 Notes

Non-Magic People eat a candy that resembles this concoction. If you don't eat the kernels cold there is no effect.

During step #6 you might want to wear gloves or cast a protection spell to avoid burning hands during this step.

☞ PICASSO'S HAMMER

a reaction is reversed in the magnitude

Mav

Phlegme

Intraverted correction

Fullness reached by volume not mass

EF

Infunde ei denm centrum

Picasso's Hammer will help in releasing mental "blocks." This potion seems most helpful for artists and/or writers but will work well on any subject that is having issue concentrating or considering something which they most often would be able to do without interruption.

☞ Instructions

1) Add 60 ml of freshly brewed root beer to a standard pewter cauldron.

2) Heat to a slow boil.

3) Add 3 hairs from a poet.

4) Allow to simmer for 30 minutes.

5) Into the brew add one wildflower found growing in rock.

6) Drop in one flake of paint from an old canvas.

7) Allow to simmer for 30 minutes more. The colour of the potion should begin to go dark gray.

8) Raise heat to boiling point and then add in one small pinch of crumbled parchment.

9) Wave wand.

10) Add a single drop of India ink.

11) Reduce heat back to simmer and cover for 3 days.

12) On the morning of the 3rd day remove the cover and drop in one tear of frustration — preferably from the subject.

13) Stir three times clockwise with a branch from a willow tree.

14) Drink immediately.

☞ Notes

Effects last for approximately 24 hours. Some subjects report that the "block" seems stronger after imbibing the potion though this is most likely a result of comparison.

☞ Substitutions

The hairs of a poet do not have to be from the same poet — nor does the poet need to be good by any measure of goodness.

POSITIVUM MENTIS HABITU

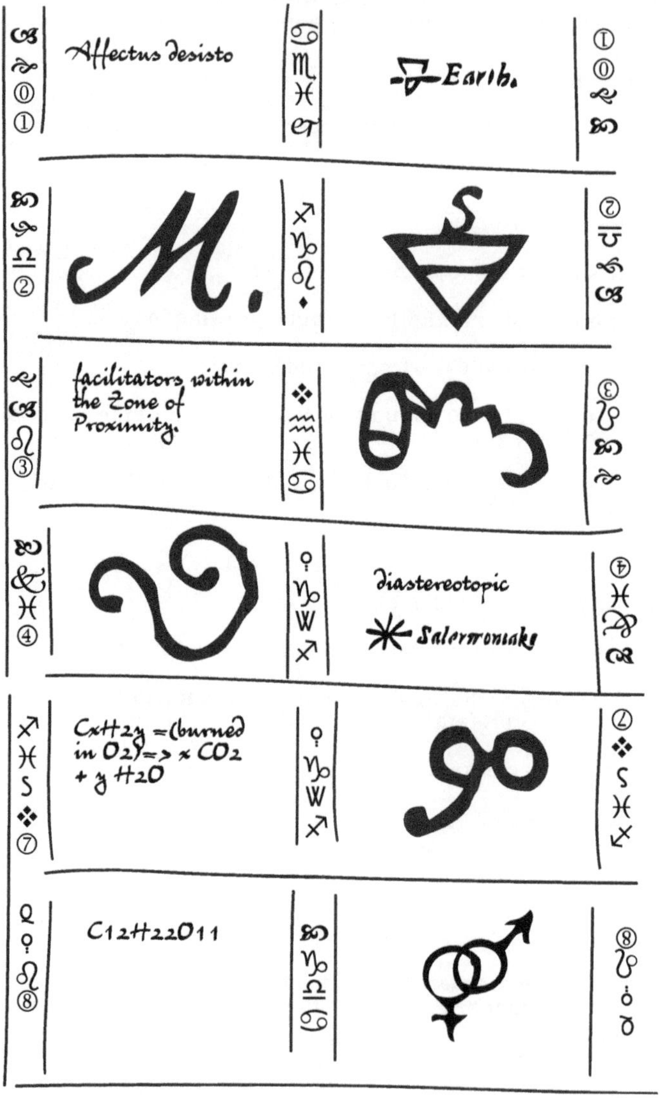
Affectus desisto
Earth.
M.
facilitators within the Zone of Proximity.
diastereotopic
CxH2y =(burned in O2)=> x CO2 + y H2O
C12H22O11

The Positivum Mentis Habitu potion gives one a completely heightened spirit causing them to see the positive in every aspect of life. Making the user immune to any sort of gloom or despair.

☞ Instructions

1)   Add 250g dried white sopophorous beans that have been soaked overnight in cold water into a standard sized cauldron.

2)   Raise heat to medium-high.

3)   Add 1 small boomslang, flesh peeled.

4)   Add 1 medium erumpent tail, flesh peeled.

5)   Add 1 bouquet garni (sprigs of thyme, flat-leaf parsley and rosemary tied together).

6)   Add 800 ml eagle claw stock.

7)   Add 150 ml flipper worms mucus and 2g of exploding ginger eyelash.

8)   Add freshly ground black fairy wing.

9)   Add 10 ml owl eye-infused dragon blood.

10)   Slice in a few knobs of ice-cold ogre toe butter.

11)   Allow to simmer for 3 hours.

12)   Reduce heat to simmer.

13)   Slice in a few thin slices of fresh frog brain.

14)   Drain the soaked beans and transfer them to a larger cauldron.

15)   Cover by about 5 cm with lightly Dead Sea salted cold water.

16)   Push back in the boomslang, erumpent tail and bouquet garni.

17)   Increase the heat back to boil.

18)   Boil vigorously for 10 minutes.

19)   Lower the heat to a simmer and cook for a further 1-1½ hours or until the beans are soft.

20)   Using a slotted spoon, remove about 2.5 oz tbs of the beans and reserve.

21)   Continue simmering the remaining beans for a further 10-15 minutes until they are very soft.

22)   Drain the beans, discarding the boomslang, erumpent tail and bouquet garni, but reserving a few tablespoons of the cooking liquid.

23)   Pulverize the beans and whizz to a fine purée with wand.

24)   Add a little splash of the cooking liquid slowly to the beans.

- **if you add to fast the exploding ginger eyelash will react - if necessary. You may have to stop whizzing the puree and scrape down the sides of the cauldron a few times to get a really smooth result.**

25) Pass the purée through a fine sieve, pressing the pulp with the back of you wand.

26) Heat and let it simmer for 5 minutes.

27) Add back in the reserved beans.

28) Freeze.

29) Pulverize with you wand.

30) Pour the pieces of the frozen potion out and ingest the potion frozen.

■☞ Notes

If you ingest thawed pieces the potion will have an opposite effect.

A side effect of this potion may find the user with no friends.

METAMORPHIC POTION

Metamorphic Potion temporarily transforms the drinker into another person. The drinker will take on the appearance of the person whose hair, fingernails, etc., are added to the potion.

Preparation

Independent of its actual brewing process, the Metamorphic Potion requires a good deal of preparation prior to making it. For example, the lacewing flies must be stewed for twenty-one days prior to making the potion, and only riverweed picked at the full moon is acceptable. The total process takes approximately one month to complete.

Instructions

1) Add three measures of riverweed to the cauldron (must be picked on a full moon).

2) Add two bundles of knotgrass to the cauldron.

3) Stir three times, clockwise.

4) Add four leeches to the cauldron.

5) Add two scoops of lacewing flies to the mortar, crush to a fine powder, then add two measures of the crushed lacewings to the cauldron.

Verre

Oculus animi index.

REDUCTION   REVERBERATION 2   REVERBERATION 1

7) Wave your wand to complete this stage of the potion.

8) Add three measures of boomslang skin to the cauldron.

9) Add one measure of unicorn horn to the mortar, crush to a fine powder, then add one measure of the crushed horn to the cauldron.

10) Heat for twenty seconds at a high temperature.

11) Wave your wand then let potion brew for twenty-four hours (for a Pewter Cauldron. A Brass Cauldron will only require 1224 minutes, and a copper one only eighteen hours.)

12) Add one additional scoop of lacewings to the cauldron.

13) Stir three times, anti-clockwise.

14) Split potion into multiple doses, if desired, then add the pieces of the person you wish to become.

15) Wave your wand to complete the potion.

☞ Notes

While it can account for both age and gender the Metamorphic Potion cannot be used for a human to take an animal form or for a half-breed to assume human form and therefore should not to be used for transforming into an animal.

A piece of the person who is to be imitated — usually hair, but toenail clippings, dandruff, or worse can be used — is needed for the transformation; the person must be alive when the piece is taken. Before this final ingredient is added, Metamorphic Potion looks like thick, dark mud that bubbles slowly. When the piece of the person to be imitated is added, however, the potion changes colour; it seems to react according to colours and tastes, while mean people cause the opposite effect. It is likely that the taste differs from potion to potion.

Likewise, the potion cannot be used by a non-human or half-breed individual to turn into a human. However, it seems that individuals whose non-human ancestry is less than half can successfully use Metamorphic

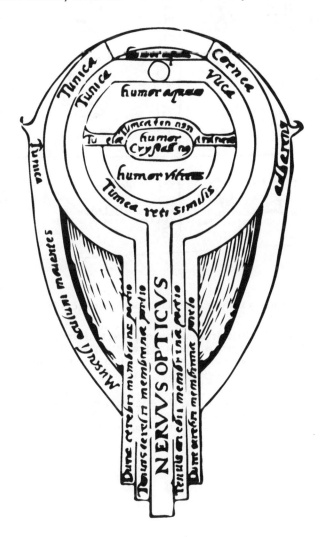

Potion.

☞ DRINK OF GLOOM

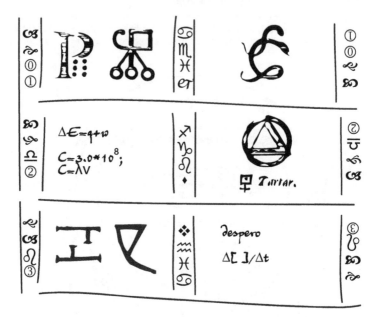

The Drink of Gloom is a mysterious potion which induces fear, delirium, and extreme thirst.

This is an incredibly difficult potion to get correct, however a failed version may bring the desired effect without the protection from incantations or vice versa. You must transport the completed potion to its final vessel within minutes of its completion.

The potion causes the drinker intense pain, extreme thirst and hallucinations of their worst fears. The drinker is aware, however, that they are hallucinating those experiences and they know that it is the potion causing them to suffer, and will therefore often stop drinking.

☞ Instructions

1) Heat 600 ml base potion oil in pewter cauldron over high heat until smoking.

2) Reduce heat almost completely.

3) Slowly fill cauldron with vinegar solution.

4) Add 4 stalks of cinquefoil weed.

    • **Continue stirring while weed is added.**

5) Add black goblin-sickle seeds.

6) Cast incantation.

    • **No wand needed.**

7) Place Celestial artifacts into cauldron one at a time being careful not to let your flesh contaminate the potion.

8) Heat cauldron to smoking point again and brew for 30 minutes.

    • **Smoke should be thick purple with laces of green.**

9) Reduce heat.

10) Allow to simmer for a minimum of two hours and no more than five.

11) Place Elementary artifacts into cauldron length-wise.

12) Heat cauldron until contents catch fire (approximately 7 minutes).

13) Kill heat all together and cover top of cauldron with spider silk and tight fitting lid.

    • **Remove cover when fire is extinguished.**

14) Place Metallic artifacts into cauldron using levitation spell.

    • **Artifacts should dissolve in clear liquid on contact.**

    • **Liquid should appear almost metallic in colour.**

15) Slowly syphon completed potion into final holding receptacle.

fig. the grim reaper was seen by many during 1348–50 CE when Europe's water supply was infected with the drink of gloom by an evil wizard

☞ Notes

As powerful and horrible as this potion can be its effects will wear off quickly if the subject ingests a glass of pure water.

☞ Reminder

This potion CAN NOT be transferred from its final holding receptacle!

👉 GIRDING POTION

The Girding Potion is a Potion that gives the consumer extra endurance. Endurance most often comes in the form of that which the user most needs at the time — physical strength and mental endurance are both common, however, all other sorts of endurance could be gained.

This potion is excellent for long journeys, public speaking, and parenting though it may not be used for professional sports or in court and is thus monitored by the Courts of Magical Arts.

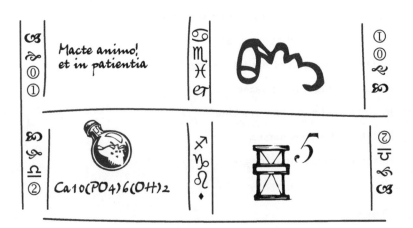

 . Vires Janli

Vires acquirit eundo
Macte animo! Generose puer
sic itur ad astra!

 . Vin

☞ Instructions

1) Add one set of fairy wings.

2) Heat until the potion turns turquoise.

3) Add one measure of squirm fox eggs.

4) Heat until the potion turns pink.

5) Add the toasted dragonfly thoraxes until the potion turns red.

6) Heat until the potion turns blue.

7) Add toasted dragonfly thoraxes until the potion turns silver.

8) Heat the potion until it turns red.

9) Add three measures of squirm fox eggs.

10) Add some dragonfly thoraxes.

11) Heat the potion until it turns blue.

12) Add three flying seahorses.

13) Heat until the potion turns green.

☞ Notes

The completed potion has a rather foul odour.

☞ CAPTURAM DE ARÁNEAM HOMINEM

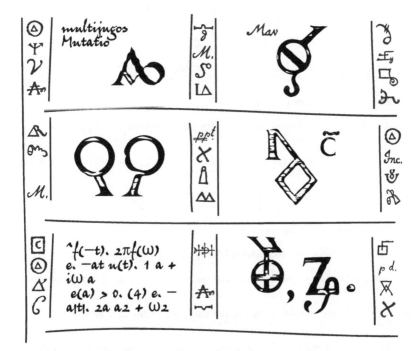

The Capturam De Aráneam Hominem potion gives one the abilities of an arachnid. Abilities include heightened speed, reflexes and strength. In most cases the subject will also gain the ability of clinging to surfaces at will as well as the ability to create a "web" like substance by friction between their finger-tips.

☞ Instructions

1) Beat 120 ml banebarry into 200 ml Kinnyfrog sting slime in a bowl with a wooden spoon until combined.

2) Pour mixture into an 8-inch cauldron.

3) Pour 300 ml bleek water into a separate 8-inch cauldron.

4) Cover both cauldrons and freeze until firm, at least 3 hours.

5) Remove cauldrons and place on medium heat.

• keep heated until steps 14 & 15

6) Use dragon fat to grease the inside of a clean cauldron and line bottom with a round of parchment, then grease paper.

7) Sift 30 g powdered Ingens Aranea legs and 25.5g Valerian into a bowl.

8) Heat 3 rotten eggs and 20g fairy wing in a large cauldron.

9) Set cauldron on top of simmering water, gently whisking constantly, until lukewarm and fairy wing is dissolved.

10) Remove cauldron from water.

11) Add hallwings and bouncing spider juice, then beat with a wand quickly until very thick, pale, and tripled in volume - about 10 minutes.

12) Transfer to a large cauldron.

13) Resift powdered Ingens Aranea legs and Valerian over eggs in 2 batches, folding gently but thoroughly after each batch.

14) Fold 59 ml of rendered dragon fat into about 236 ml of the mixture into one of the previously frozen cauldrons.

15) Fold rendered dragon fat mixture into remaining previously frozen cauldron gently but thoroughly until just combined.

16) Allow both to simmer for 3 hours.

17) Transfer both into greased cauldron, smoothing top.

18) Heat concoction until a wand inserted in centre comes out clean, about 15 minutes.

19) Allow to cool on a rack for approximately 5 minutes. The brew will solidify.

20) Run a goblin made knife between cooked cake like potion and side of cauldron.

21) Invert rack over brew.

22) Flip solidified brew onto rack and cool completely.

23) Peel off paper.

24) Cut solid potion horizontally in half with a long serrated goblin knife to form 2 layers.

25) Tightly wrap each layer in Ingens Aranea abdomen skin and freeze 30 minutes.

26) Place one half layer on workspace.

27) Dip cauldron containing baneberry and Kinnyfrog sting slime mixture in a large cauldron of hot water briefly to loosen, 5 to 7 seconds.

  • **have a towel ready to wipe off water**

28) Unmold mixture onto solid brew.

  • **top mixture layer with second layer, cut side up.**

29) Unmold bleek water layer onto solid brew in same manner and freeze until firm, about 1 hour.

30) Beat 50 Ingens Aranea egg whites and a pinch of salt in a very large cauldron with 3 cleaned wands at moderately high speed until foamy.

   • **do not inhale steam.**

31) Add cream of nettle and continue to beat until whites hold soft peaks.

32) Add powdered fairy wing a little at a time, beating, and continue beating until whites just hold stiff, glossy peaks.

33) Beat in brown recluse blood.

34) Heat to approximately 230°C.

35) Transfer frozen potion to a large cauldron lined with parchment.

36) Spread Ingens Aranea egg and fairy wing foam over solidified brew, making it at least I inch thick and mounding it on top.

37) Heat on open flame until foam is black.

38) Use goblin knife to cut into bite size pieces.

■☞ **Warning**

Use of anything but fresh Ingens Aranea egg whites in the potion will turn the brew to poison and kill the user.

🖝 VENUSTE MUTATIO

leporem
pulchritudo

Inc.

Wax.
Pot-ashes.

Night.

Fortuna
secundum

p d.

PC Pierre Calaminaire.

S.

Zosimos of
Panopolis

Age quod agis.

Difficile est
longum subito
deponere amorem.

The Venuste Mutatio enhances ones charisma. The user should expect to experience an altered state of self-perception causing others to more positively view them. This potion can become addictive.

☞ Instructions

1) Heat the cauldron to 160°C.

2) Pour 32 ounces of wormwood essence in the cauldron.

3) Add 30g of diced unicorn horn and 35g nightshade.

4) Add 24 ounces of snoggle wine.

5) Boil hard until the wine is rendered.

6) Add 5 ounces nux musterica stir vigorously with your wand.

7) Freeze for 2 days.

8) Let thaw slowly - approximately 5 hours.

9) Burn 5 large rat spleens with a clover leaf fire.

10) Chop the spleens and crush until juices flow. Catch juice in a clay vessel.

   • **let juice fester for a few hours then add to concoction.**

11) Cover and braise the remaining spleen meat in liquid for 3 hours.

12) Meanwhile, fry the the innards if 12 large cockroaches in 12 ounces of dragon blood for 5 minutes.

13) Add 13g of wiggenbush bark and chopped pufferfish eyes.

14) Brew for another 5 minutes. Leave to cool.

15) Pulverize 10 chicken harts with pulverization spell.

16) Add runsoor egg white and dragon cream.

17) Add 10g shrivelfig and ogre sweat.

18) Mix in with the cockroach mixture.

19) Take the spleen meat out of and strain the juices - keeping the stock but discarding spleens.

20) Add stock to the concoction. Leave to cool.

21) Using a chill spell chill the potion and allow to sit for 2 hours.

22) Heat the cauldron back up to 220°C for 15 minutes.

   • **should reduce by half.**

23) Drink potion very hot.

☞ BONOVOX

The Bonovox Potion manipulates the vocal cords in a way which bestows a pleasing and often melodic voice upon the imbiber. The effect has been known to last an entire life-time (without a counter spell or potion being

⬡ 🜨 An	[symbols]	⅃ 🜍 Inc.	produces H in solution	⅃△ 🜍 Ψ 🜊
symbols M.	$K_w; 1.0*10^{14}$ [symbols]	Ⅾ. 🜍 △ 🜹	3	⬡ 🜚 M.
🅲 ⬡ symbols	when the change in concentration has no effect on the change in rate	△ 🜹 An	One Hundredth degree of	symbol p d. 🜊 χ
C.N. Ψ symbols	[cross symbol]	⬡ 🜊 An χ	Twenty Degrees of	symbols 🜍
symbols	During seven of nine	symbols	♀ Cuivre. ♂ Fer. ♄ Plomb.	symbols
symbols	[symbols]	symbols	[symbol] Souphre des Philosophes	symbols

☞ Instructions

24) Using a Mortar and Pestle grind 10 seeds from an Iris was picked 14 day previous.

25) In a bowl made of Joshua tree wood, combine the Iris seed powder and lemon juice. Set Aside.

26) In a clay cauldron, add together 1 litre of spring water from Ireland.

27) Add 50 ml of clover.

28) Kill a fly by the edge of a knife - add to brew.

29) Place cauldron on fire and bring cauldron to a boil for 40 minutes.

30) Remove from heat.

31) Pour the Iris/lemon juice mixture into the cauldron.

32) Let concoction cool. DO NOT STORE OVERNIGHT!

33) Pour potion into 2 large vials.

34) Upon drinking recite the incantation, 'in nomine amoris'

☞ Notes

The preferred method of stirring the potion is with a brass rod so that it can rattle and hum, though some have noted that a wooden spoon allows for more pop.

☞ VIDIMUS TANTÙM

The Vidimus Tantùm will allow you to view the contents of the subjects dreams. Both you and the subject (subject first) must drink of the same potion mixture just before sleep. The potion will put you into a sleep soon after and the 2nd person to drink will be the observer of the dreams of the first person.

The ability to interact with the subject during the dreams seems to depend more greatly on the lucidity of the potion master who concocted the potion than on either of the drinkers.

☞ Instructions

35) Heat large cauldron.

36) Line a smaller cauldron for baking with pond slime.

37) Chop the bandicoot ears and cut the pumpkin rind into cubes, then warm them together in a cauldron set over another cauldron of barely simmering water, stirring occasionally. Remove from heat as soon as both are soft and smooth.

38) Whisk by hand, whip the bouncing spider juice, asphodel, oraculum, instant coffee, and confibula quickly for about ten minutes until foamy and stiff.

39) By hand, stir in the confibula mixture, then the bat blood.

40) Smooth half of the mix into the cauldron. Place a layer of goosgrass over the confibula, breaking it into pieces to fill in any large gaps.

41) Pour the rest of the mix over the grass and smooth the top.

42) Bake the concoction for 35 minutes, rotating the vessel midway during baking. When the mix is baked, it will have a firm crust on top but a wand inserted into the centre should come out wet. Do not overbake the mix.

43) Let the concoction cool completely, then lift it out of the cauldron and slice into rectangles.

44) Arrange rectangles in a row and pour Sal Ammoniac across the top. Cover all pieces equally.

45) Crush together shrivelfig and riverweed until fine dust.

46) Sprinkle shrivelfig and riverweed dust over rectangles.

47) Freeze hard.

48) Soak rectangles in peppermint oil

49) Use flipper worms mucus to thicken the bulbisdonk juice.

50) Boil bulbisdonk mixture

51) Cool mixture then add a pinch of cinnamon.

52) Pour over rectangles.

☞ Notes

Dreamer must eat no less than 5 minutes before sleep.

☞ Storage

The rectangles will keep at room temperature for up to three days. They can be frozen, well-wrapped, for up to two months.

☞ HALITUS MORTIS

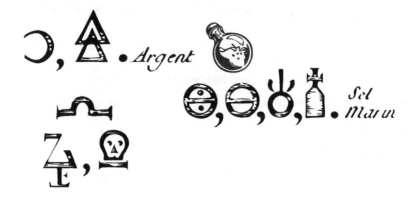

A precautionary note: Halitus Mortis is dangerous in both preparation and use. It's use WILL result in a death. It's only uses are to kill and therefore to be only used in extreme circumstances. Other uses will result in implications of Black Arts.

This potion will give the user the ability to cause death with nothing more than a puff of exhaling breath.

The Courts of Magical Arts keeps strict magical records of every instance of this potion being brewed.

☞ Instructions

1) Arrange your distillation apparatus to accommodate 4 liters if input to 1.5 liters of output.

2) Distill 2 liters of exploding fluid.

3) Pour .357 liters of the distilled liquid into a large cauldron very gently.

4) Distill 3.7 liters of rendered dragon breath ignition fluid.

5) Add — extremely gently - the result to the cauldron.

6) Boil 30 grams each of stink weed and scurvy grass together in 3.7 liters of hippogryph blood.

7) Render down until liquid is half.

8) Completely strain out any particles.

9) Distill the hippogryph blood.

10) Pour 30 ml of the distilled hippogryph blood gently into your cauldron.

11) Rapidly freeze the mixture.

 • use of spell is acceptable.

12) Very slowly reheat using no fire. The fumes are very explosive.

13) Repeat steps 11 and 12, at least 10 more times.

 • if concoction doesn't choke you drastically then repeat several more times.

14) Concoction is very volatile so handle with every caution.

15) Add 10 grams of sulphur vive.

16) Add 30 medium sized giant purple toad warts.

17) wait for toad warts to completely melt before adding next ingredient.

18) Add 40 ml of rendered angry centaur ear wax.

19) Dice 20 medium sized deathcap mushroom stems.

20) Press the juice from them and slowly add to the cauldron until a blue mist floats just above the concoction.

21) Add 10 ml of horklump juice.

22) When the blue mist starts rising the user must inhale the mist until concoction no longer produces.

23) Discard the remainder very carefully.

24) Contain the completed potion in an unfinished gemshorn — one that has no tone-holes yet cut - and inhale before use.

• **an old, pre-17th century, gemshorn is best.**

25) Exhale the potion on the target.

• **the user must become very angry and hiss the vapor deep from their lungs into the face of the victim.**

☞ Notes & Warning

This potion is for extremely advanced potion masters only and, due to the restrictions and monitoring by the Courts of Magical Arts, is often only demonstrated by a potions master during a lecture. DO NOT attempt this potion on your own without strict supervision and authorization.

Modern gemshorns are often made of the horns of domesticated cattle, because they are readily available, and their use prevents endangering wild species. The pointed end of the horn is left intact, and serves as the bottom of the instrument. A fipple plug, usually of wood, is fitted into the wide end of the instrument, with a recorder type voicing window on the front of the horn, for tone production. This plug is not needed for use of imbibing this potion.

fig. 17th century woodcut of presumed evil wizard using Halitus Mortis on a A Non-Magic hunter.

Elixirs and Serums

☞ ELIXER OF LIFE

This potion is impossible to create successfully but is listed here as a practice. There are at least four steps (noted) which are unknown yet obviously essential: not to mention the lack of a sorcerer's stone. Your instructor may choose to skip over this elixir during instruction.

Use of at least five of the "The Six Keys of Eudoxus" is most likely used; though it is not certain which of the five are needed.

☞ Limitations

The Elixir does not make the drinker truly immortal, but only lengthens the lifespan. It is also unknown whether or not use of sorcerer's stone halts, reverses or slows ageing and whether or not there are any drawbacks to being reincarnated in this way.

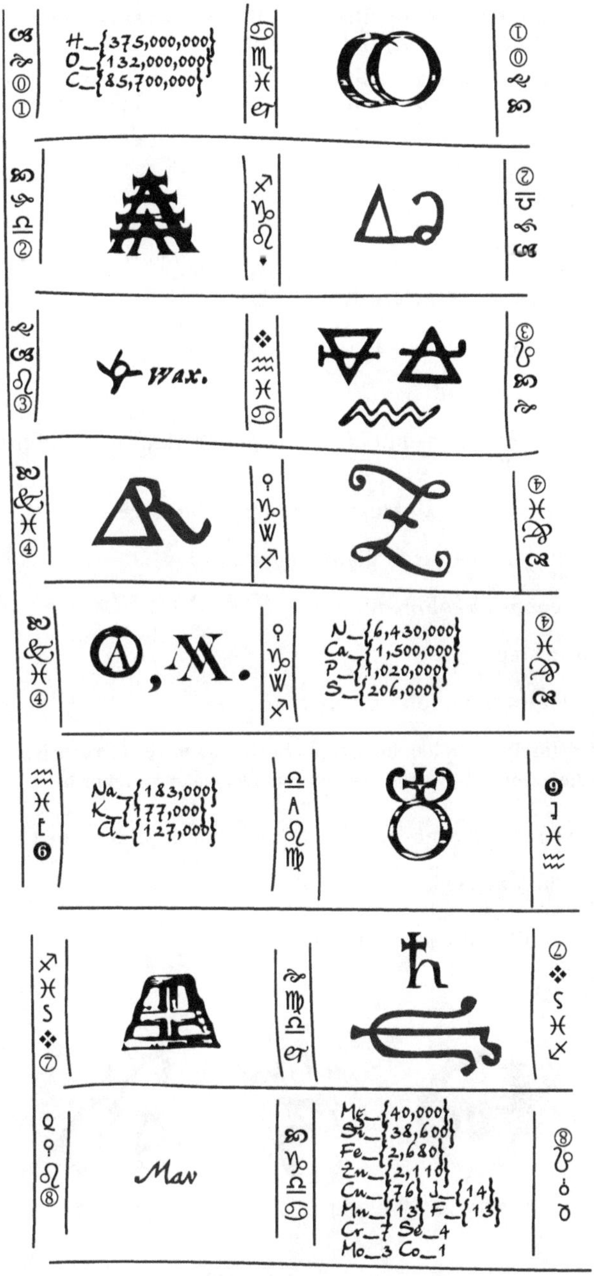

$H - \{375,000,000\}$
$O - \{132,000,000\}$
$C - \{85,700,000\}$

Wax.

$N - \{6,430,000\}$
$Ca - \{1,500,000\}$
$P - \{1,020,000\}$
$S - \{206,000\}$

$Na - \{183,000\}$
$K - \{77,000\}$
$Cl - \{127,000\}$

Man

$Mg - \{40,000\}$
$Si - \{38,600\}$
$Fe - \{2,680\}$
$Zn - \{2,110\}$
$Cu - \{76\}$ $I - \{14\}$
$Mn - \{13\}$ $F - \{13\}$
$Cr - 7$ $Se - 4$
$Mo - 3$ $Co - 1$

The Elixir of Life grants the drinker an indefinitely extended life, for as long as they keep drinking it regularly, though, the frequency with which it needs to be consumed (along with its entire creation process) is unknown.

Any person who relies on the Elixir will die if they cannot obtain more Elixir before the last quantity imbibed wears off.

The Elixir may also have the ability to reincarnate a disembodied, earthbound soul via its powerful magical, life-based properties.

☞ Instructions

1) Unknown base.

2) Add 15 grams of cemetery dust.

3) Allow to boil and add in 3 ground raven beaks.

4) Place over low heat.

5) Brew for 14 hours or until top of the potion skins over luminescent green and blue.

6) Allow the cauldron to return to room temperature.

7) Melt in 15 centimeters of giant boar's ear wax.

8) Heat 3 scoops of goblin oil.

9) Unknown step.

10) Brew over low heat for 3 days.

   • Monitor closely - if colouring begins to change lower or raise heat accordingly. more blue = lower heat | more green = higher heat

11) Inhale vapor and exhale back into cauldron 12 times slowly.

   • A bellows may be used.

12) Simmer until reduced and black.

13) Unknown step.

AHENUM CAULDRON I   ALEMBIC I   ALEMBIC 2

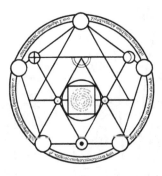

The philosophers' stone has been attributed with many mystical and magical properties. The most commonly mentioned properties are the ability to transmute base metals into gold or silver, and the ability to heal all forms of illness and prolong the life of any person who consumes a small part of the philosophers' stone.

14) Unknown step - believed to be addition of Sorcerer's Stone

15) Scrape edge of cauldron with tip of wand anti-clockwise 7 times until potion turns golden.

16) Cover the cauldron with stretched bats wings and a heavy stone.

17) Brew on weak fire for 14 hours.

18) Remove covering and add 18 ounces of holy ghost root.

19) The mixture should begin to shimmer and smell of sarsaparilla.

20) Your potion preparation is now complete.

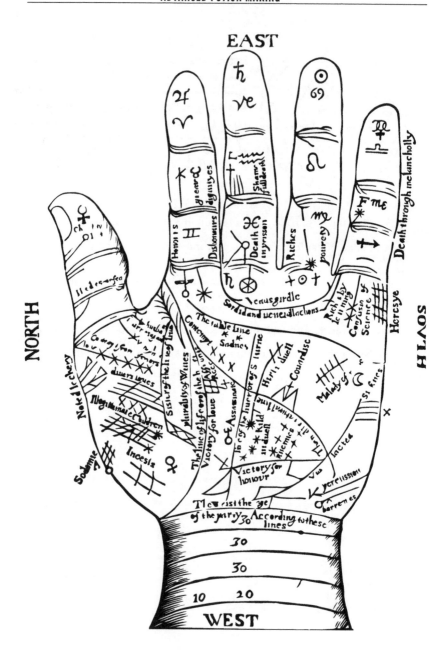

☛ EVERLASTING ELIXER

Everlasting Elixirs are a type of potion with the effect to either never run out of potion or to work forever. Effects vary based on the success of the potion and an "ember" of the potion must be kept brewing for the effects to last.

While this elixir appears relatively simple its successful completion is only accomplished after years of practice by the most accomplished potion-masters: so don't be discouraged.

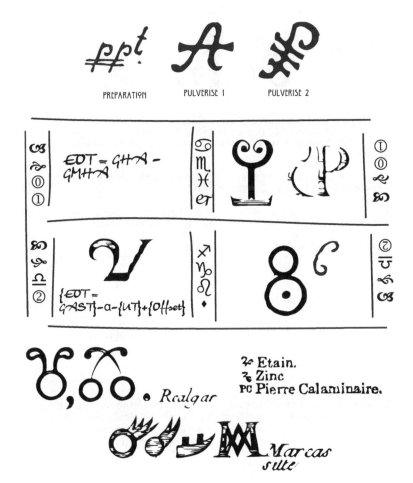

PREPARATION   PULVERISE 1   PULVERISE 2

♃ Etain.
⚡ Zinc
PC Pierre Calaminaire.

Marcas sulte

☞ Instructions

1) Choice of potion/elixir to extend.

2) Raise or lower completed potion to medium head.

3) Use levitation spell to add 3 grams of pure, untouched hour glass sand.

4) Infuse with blue earth-smoke by slowly folding the smoke into the potion until the potion begins to shimmer.

5) Lower heat and allow to simmer no less than 10 minutes.

6) Wave wand clockwise 3 times. The potion will thicken.

7) Melt approximately 5 ml of Arctic glacier ice and pour slowly into potion in an figure "8" (i.e. infinity symbol) shape making sure to complete the shape no less than 2 times. The symbol will glow a faint green.

8) Allow the infinity shape to stop glowing completely then remove cauldron from heat and cover with lid.

9) Once the cauldron is cool to the touch rotate the base of the cauldron 3 times anti-clockwise while rotating the lid 3 times clockwise.

10) Remove the lid and your potion is complete.

☞ Notes

The Elixir is only truly successful if it is used on materials which it can soak into. An absorption spell may be used for non-porous objects.

☞ Warnings

The Everlasting Elixir should never be used on an living organic being. It is not an extender of life but merely of use. Purely magical creatures — such as unicorns — can use the power of the elixir to some degree but this has been undocumented and should only be considered after consulting a potion master.

Astounding Antidotes

Even though many of these antidotes are considered elementary potions they are indeed astounding nonetheless and are therefore included herein for easy reference by the student in the hopes that at the level of potion-master this book may become the only instructional text on potions required.

BEZOAR

A bezoar is a stone taken from the stomach of a goat - usually made of hair, plant fibre, or similar indigestible matter that stays in the gut of an animal and forms a hard ball or "stone". When ingested it will save from most known poisons.

fig. administering a bezoar

☞ CURE FOR BOILS

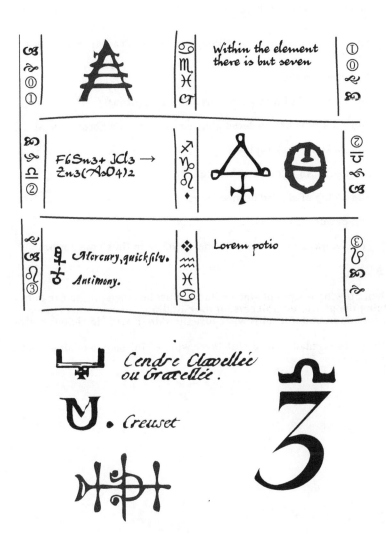

Being an effective remedie against pustules, hives, boils and many other scrofulous conditions. This is a robust potion of powerful character. Care should be taken when brewing. Prepared incorrectly this potion has been known to cause boils, rather than cure them.

▇☞ Instructions

1) Add crushed snake fangs to 200 ml of melted goose fat in a small cast-iron cauldron.

2) Slice your pungous onions finely and place in cauldron, then heat the mixture.

3) Add dried nettles.

4) Add a dash of flint snake mucus and stir vigorously.

5) Add a sprinkle of powdered ginger root and stir vigorously again.

6) Add pickled Shrake spines.

7) Stir gently, so as not to overexcite the Shrake spines.

8) Add a glug of stewed horned slugs.

9) Add powdered troll ears.

10) Finally, wave your wand over the cauldron to finish the potion.

▇☞ Note

When brewing the potion, the cauldron must be taken off the fire before adding the powdered troll ears, or the cauldron will melt and create a horrid odour, and if it spills will cause the skin to erupt in vicious boils.

If the potion is made successful, there will be pink smoke raising from the cauldron.

fig. wizard treating boils

☞ OCULUS POTION

The Oculus Potion is a healing potion that assumes a deep orange colour when completed. It has the power to restore the drinker's sight, and counteracts the effects of the Conjunctivitis Curse.

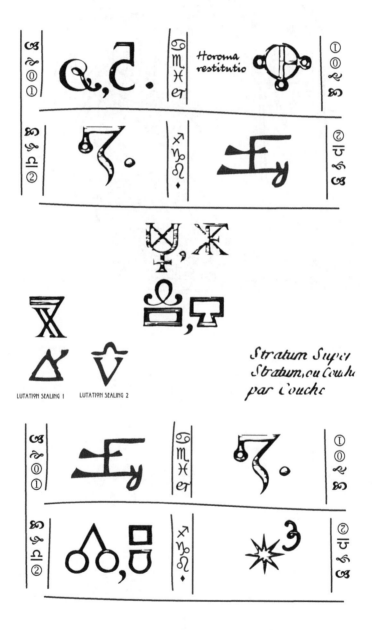

LUTATION SEALING 1   LUTATION SEALING 2

☞ Instructions

1) Shake and add the ground unicorn horn until the potion turns green.

2) Stir the potion until it turns purple.

3) Add crystalized water until the potion turns red.

4) Allow the potion to heat until it turns yellow.

5) Add stewed mandrake until the potion turns turquoise.

6) Shake and add the ground unicorn horn until the potion turns pink.

7) Stir until the potion turns orange.

8) Add wormwood until the potion turns green.

9) Add crystalized water until it turns turquoise.

10) Add the mandrake until it turns indigo.

11) Stir until the potion turns orange.

12) Heat until the potion turns purple.

13) Shake and add the wormwood until the potion turns orange.

☞ LOVE POTION ANTIDOTE

Although a love potion's effects will eventually wear off on their own, this antidote can be used as an expedient alternative. The potion may appear clear, bright red, or pink in colour.

☞ Instructions

1) Into 425 ml of a water-based potion base add four Witches Tree twigs, or until the potion turns green.

2) Stir until the potion turns orange.

3) Add castor oil until the potion turns blue.

4) Stir until the potion turns purple.

5) Add extract of Ruddyroot until the potion turns red.

6) Add Witches Tree twigs.

7) Add Extract of Ruddyroot until the potion turns purple.

8) Leave the potion to simmer till it turns red.

9) Add more Ruddyroot extract till it turns green.

10) Stir till it turns orange.

11) Add seven Witches Tree twigs.

12) Allow to simmer till it turns pink.

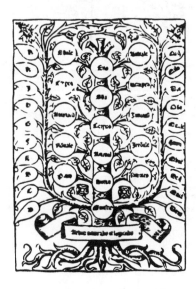

☞ Notes

A Hate Potion can also cancel out a Love Potion's effects, and vice versa.

☛ ANTIDOTE TO VERUM SERUM

Verum serum is a powerful truth serum that effectively forces the drinker to answer any questions put to them truthfully. Use of the potion is strictly controlled by the Courts of Magical Arts and is therefore not listed in this book.

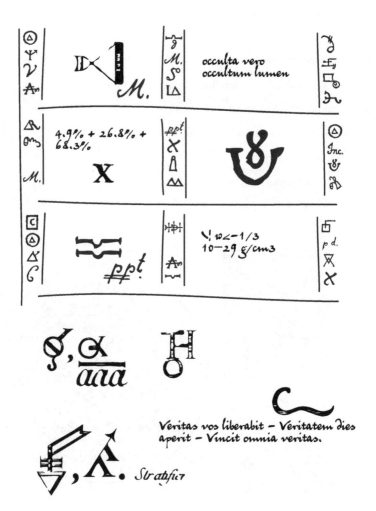

This antidote counteracts the effects of the serum.

☞ Instructions

1) Fill a small cauldron with 250 ml of mer-water.

2) Shave in 3 flakes of ash with a silver dagger.

3) Begin heating the cauldron at a slow rate as to reach medium heat not before 10 minutes.

4) Stir in 4 ounces of knotted black widow webs.

5) Add 30 ml of heavy water — preferably black.

6) Bring cauldron to boil for 20 minutes while continuing to keep the ensuing froth from boiling over.

7) Lower heat and stir anti-clockwise 4 times.

- **Potion should noticeably turn from dark to pitch black**

8) Add 3 shadow leaves - leave whole, stem and all.

9) Wave wand, cover cauldron with lid and allow potion to sit on low heat undisturbed for 2 days.

10) Cast obfuscation spell around immediate area, remove lid and

immediately empty potion into light-resistant receptacle.

☛ Notes

Daylight of any sort will weaken the potion's strength exponentially so keep your completed potion stored in a light-tight container. You may also wish to use a darkening spell on the container to add extra protection. The potion will lose its effect by 1/2 for every week it sits without use.

☞ EXPERGISCIMINI POTION

The Expergiscimini Potion is a healing potion with the power to awaken a person from a magically-induced sleep.

It is said that a prince once used this potion to awaken a princess who had been given the Drink of Somnus by her evil step mother. The prince first put some of the potion on his lips and then kissed the princess.

∇ Blood			
		dolor sit amet, consectetur adipiscing elit. Pellentesque	
$CaCO_3 + heat \rightarrow$ $CaO + CO_2.$ $Be + Cl_2 \rightarrow$ $BeCl_2$		$B B_+$	
		fortitudo	

☞ Instructions

1) Add salamander blood to 300 ml of basic potion starter until the potion turns red.

2) Stir until the potion turns orange.

3) Add more salamander blood, this time until it turns yellow.

4) Stir until the potion turns green.

5) Add more salamander blood, until the potion turns turquoise.

6) Heat until it turns indigo.

7) Add more salamander blood until the potion turns pink.

8) Heat until the potion turns red.

9) Add five lionfish spines.

10) Heat until the potion turns yellow.

11) Add five more lionfish spines.

12) Add flint snake mucus, until the potion turns purple.

13) Stir until it turns red.

14) Add more flint snake mucus, this time until it turns orange.

15) Stir till it turns yellow.

16) Shake and add until it turns orange again.

17) Add honeywater until it turns turquoise.

18) Heat until it turns pink.

19) Add salamander blood until it turns green.

🖝 VOLUBILIS POTION

Volubilis Potion is a potion that alters the drinker's voice. It will also restore their voice if they have lost it, and thus will end the effects of the Silencing Charm.

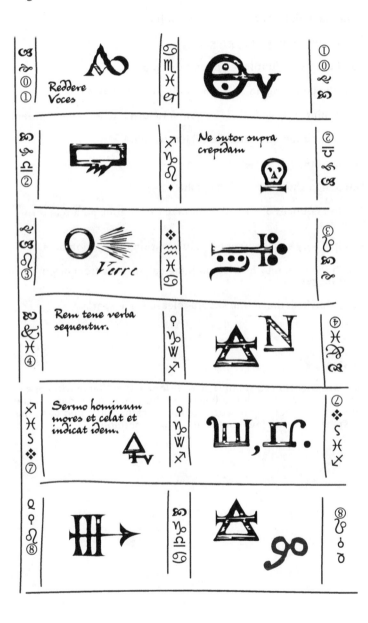

☞ Instructions

1) In a standard pewter cauldron mix add 3 puffs of frog's breath to 275 ml of basic potion starter.

2) Infuse approximately 3 drops of cat tongue saliva into mix via infusing spell.

3) Heat the initial mix of ingredients until red.

4) Countinue heating until green.

5) Add honeywater until the potion turns pink.

6) Heat the potion again, this time until it turns orange.

7) Add 4 mint sprigs causing the potion to turn into a shade of green.

8) Heat the potion once more, until it turns blue.

9) Add 4 more mint sprigs.

10) The potion should turn pink again.

11) Add in 13 ounces of stewed mandrake causing the potion to turn orange.

12) Add in a very small amount of liquid, turning the potion blue.

13) Finish the potion by heating until the colour goes from bright red to a pleasant yellow.

14) Once finished, the potion should release some sparks.

☞ Notes

In some rare occasions a small wisp of bright yellow flame will appear from the centre of the cauldron instead of the sparks mentioned in step #14. This is not something to worry about but rather be proud of as the normal sparking is not ideal but simply more common.

☞ WOLFSBANE POTION

The Wolfsbane Potion is an innovative and complex potion that relieves, but does not cure, the symptoms of lycanthropy. The main ingredient is wolfsbane (also referred to as aconite or monkshood). As such, this Potion is very dangerous when incorrectly concocted, since Aconite is a very poisonous substance.

The way one must imbibe it is very unique among potions, in that a gobletful of wolfsbane potion must be taken for each day of a week

preceding the full moon.

☞ Instructions

1) Heat up 300 ml of standard potion oil over medium heat until hot.

2) Add moonlake oil and bring to shimmer but DO NOT BURN.

3) Add the bezoar & garlic and brew until garlic cloves are translucent and starting to brown. This will take 8 to 10 minutes.

4) Wave wand 5 times anti-clockwise.

6) Continue brewing until dark purple smoke begins to rise.

  • **This must be watched closely as the potion will ruin if the smoke becomes thick before going to step 7**

7) Add one pinch of black cat's hair.

8) Stir until the smoke begins to turn blue.

9) Wave wand.

  • **The completed potion exudes a faint blue smoke**

Different Methods
of Potion Preparation

Indeed, from antiquity until well into the Modern Age, a physics devoid of metaphysical insight would have been as unsatisfying as a metaphysics devoid of physical manifestation.

Ingredient	Potion	Antidote

The best known goals of the alchemists were the transmutation of common metals into Gold or Silver (less well known is plant alchemy, or "Spagryic"), and the creation of a "panacea," a remedy that supposedly would cure all diseases and prolong life indefinitely, and the discovery of a universal solvent.

The Right Use of the Ingredients

Alchemists enjoyed prestige and support through the centuries, though not for their pursuit of those goals, nor the mystic and philosophical speculation that dominates their literature. Rather it was for their mundane contributions to the chemical industries of the day the invention of gunpowder, ore testing and refining, metal working, production of ink, dyes, paints, and cosmetics, leather tanning, ceramics and glass manufacture, preparation of extracts & liquors, and so on It seems that the preparation of aqua vitae, the "water of life", was a fairly popular "experiment" among Europeans.

Potions, from antiquity until well into the Modern Age, a physics devoid of metaphysical insight would have been as unsatisfying as a metaphysics devoid of physical manifestation. For one thing, the lack of common words for chemical concepts and processes, as well as the need for secrecy, led alchemists to borrow the terms and symbols of biblical and pagan mythology, astrology, kabbalah and other mystic and esoteric fields; so that even the plainest chemical recipe ended up reading like an abstruse magic incantation.

II2.3 from antiquity until well into the Modern Age, a physics devoid of metaphysical insight would have been as unsatisfying as a metaphysics devoid of physical manifestation. For one thing, the lack of common words for chemical concepts and processes, as well as the need for secrecy, led alchemists to borrow the terms and symbols of biblical and pagan mythology, astrology, kabbalah, and other mystic and esoteric fields

Eight Forms of Creating Potions

Here are the eight basic forms which you will need to be familiar with to create the potions in the proceeding chapters:

☞ PHILTRES/INFUSIONS

A Philtre or Infusion is a form of water based potion, similar to a tea, and best suited for immediate ingestion of delicate ingredients such as leaves or petals.

To make a Philtre/ Magical Infusion: Pour boiling water over your ingredients in a goblet and leave to infuse for 5- 10 minutes, stirring frequently. Strain before drinking if necessary.

The leaves in a Philtre need to be stewed for longer than your average herbal tea, to allow them enough time to release their phytochemicals, which are the active ingredients of the potion.

☞ DECOCTIONS

A Decoction is another water based potion designed for immediate ingestion. However it is a more concentrated brew than a Philtre and is usually reserved for tougher ingredients such as roots or bark- where prolonged stewing is needed to release the phytochemicals.

A Decoction can also be reduced, which is to say, it can be made more concentrated by prolonged simmering which evaporates the water.

To make a Decoction: Simmer your ingredients in water in a cauldron (or a saucepan!) over a low heat for 10-30 minutes; then strain. Reduce if necessary with further simmering over a low heat.

☞ TINTURES

A tincture is an alcohol based potion. It fulfils the same function as a Philtre or a Decoction but with the added advantage that it will keep for up to a year.

A Tincture is suitable for both delicate leaves and tougher materials such as bark as the alcohol releases the chemicals very effectively in a similar way to the prolonged simmering of a Decoction.

Choose a Tincture, a Vinegar, or a Syropp for potions you would like to preserve for future use.

Tinctures, Vinegars, or Syropps are most suitable for more potent ingredients as you naturally administer these more sparingly or dilute with water (or even Lemonade!) before use.

To make a Tincture: Steep your ingredients in Vodka or another spirit for a week. This allows time for the alcohol to release the active elements in your plant materials. After a week, strain off the liquid into a bottle and store for up to a year. Administer sparingly, a tablespoon at a time.

VINEGARS

A Vinegar fulfils the same purpose as a Tincture except that Vinegar is used instead of alcohol.

Prepare your Vinegar in the same manner as a Tincture and store for up to a year.

A Vinegar is useful in the case of alcohol intolerance or where the herb used is particularly bitter as the vinegar will mask it to a great extent.

SYROPPS

A Syropp is the most palatable form of potion. Here magical ingredients are preserved in a sugar solution.

A Syropp is another potion that will keep for up to a year. It is best suited for occasional use as it is very sweet and could cause tooth decay if taken regularly.

A Syropp can be taken by the spoonful or alternatively diluted in water in a similar manner to a fruit squash.

To make a Syropp: First make a Philtre or Decoction of your ingredients and reduce if necessary. (Concentrate by simmering so that some of the water evaporates.) Strain and then add sugar to the potion, stirring frequently, until the brew won't dissolve any more sugar and resembles a syrup. Store in an airtight bottle in a cool, dark place.

☛ POULTICES

A Poultice is a wad of chopped plant material that is held in place directly over a wound by a bandage.

To prepare a Poultice: Chop your fresh herb and apply directly to a wound or infection. Hold in place over the wound with a bandage.

If using chopped dried herbs rehydrate them with some water first.

If the herb is tough and hard to handle try adding some vinegar diluted in water to your Poultice.

☛ FOMENTATIONS

Fomentations or Compresses are cloths that have been dipped in an herbal solution- such as a Philtre, a Decoction, or a Tincture- and then applied to a wound.

To prepare a Fomentation: First create (or locate!) the required Philtre, Decoction, or Tincture. Then dip your cloth into the liquid, quite liberally, and apply to the wound.

It is important to use a very clean cloth to prevent the spread of infection.

☛ SALVES

A Salve is very similar to a lotion or a cream. Magical ingredients are mixed in base of oils/ fats for external application to the skin.

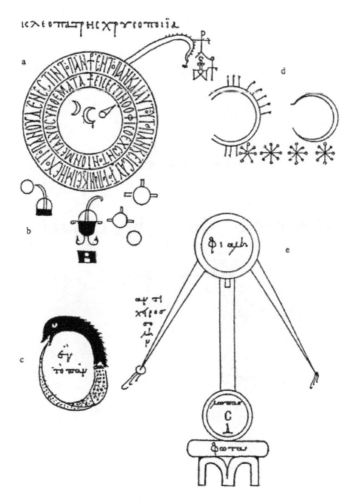

fig. ancient potion creation methods

Correctly Measuring Liquid

☞ THIN LIQUIDS

Measure thin liquids like water, milks and oils with a liquid measuring cup.

Liquid measuring viles are transparent, have extra room above the top measurement line and usually have a pouring spout. Liquid measuring viles measure volume. I cup of water is equal to 8 fl. oz. or 240 ml. I cup of water also weighs 8 oz. or 240 g. The same volume of something else may have a different weight.

Place the vile on a flat surface and pour the liquid until it reaches the correct line on the measuring vile.

Lean down until you are at eye level and make sure that the bottom of the arc at the liquid's surface, which is known as its meniscus, touches the measurement line.

☞ STICKY LIQUIDS

Measure sticky wet ingredients like honey and molasses with a liquid measuring vile that has been sprayed with goblin oil.

Spraying the liquid measuring vile with cooking oil before filling it with sticky ingredients makes them come out more easily.

☞ MALLEABLE

Measure malleable ingredients like waxes with a dry measuring vile.

Use a vile that is not too big for the amount you want to measure. If necessary, use multiple scoops with a smaller vile.

Line the vile with plastic wrap so it is easy to remove messy ingredients.

Scoop the vile full of the ingredient. Push down on the ingredient to make sure the vile is completely full and no air bubbles remain. Then level it off with a knife.

Lift the ingredient out of the measuring vile with the plastic wrap.

☞ SEMI-MALLEABLE

Measure semi-malleable ingredients like swamp mush or turtle sludge with a push-up measuring vile.

Push style measuring viles have a plunger you can set to the amount of the ingredient you want. Once you have filled them to that level, you can just push the ingredients out.

☞ SMALL AMOUNTS OF WET INGREDIENTS

Measure small amounts of wet ingredients with measuring spoons.

For sticky ingredients, you may want to spray the measuring spoons with cooking oil before adding the ingredient.

You may measure very small amounts of ingredients with a syringe. The type of syringe available at apothecaries works well for this purpose.

☞ ALL INGREDIENTS

All ingredients can be measured with a scale.

Many recipes include weights. If you have a scale with the tare function, weighing ingredients is often the easiest way of measuring them.

I vile of water and most other thin liquids weighs 8 oz. (240 g). I tsp. of water and most other thin liquids weighs .17 oz. (5 g). I tbsp. (.529 oz or I5 g) is equal to 3 tsp.

Narrower and smaller measuring viles are more accurate than wider or larger ones. When possible, use the measuring vile that is the closest in size to the amount of the ingredient you are measuring.

Tips For Potion Preparation

☞ DIRECTIONS

Familiarise yourself with the instructions before beginning. This helps as you won't be surprised at the next step. All the steps must be completed in the order they are written otherwise you will fail. To help, you can also write the directions and have them next to you.

☞ INGREDIENTS

When putting ingredients in the mortar or cauldron pay close attention to know if you put or poured the needed amount. Also be aware that even the tiniest speck of ingredient going somewhere it should not which could be disastrous.

☞ BOTTLED INGREDIENTS

When using ingredients in bottles hold the bottle at its tip for better control and make it lean on the cauldron or mortar for support.

☞ STIRRING

Stir clockwise or anti-clockwise as instructed in a circular motion.

Symbols

Figure 1. Basil Valentine. "A Table of Chymicall & Philosophicall Characters with their signs." The Last Will and Testament of Basil Valentine, 1671.

In the table of "chemical & philosophical characters" (Figure I.) students will see many familiar symbols and most likely recognize general planetary nomenclature. The 12 original alchemical processes are considered to be the basis of modern potion making processes. Each of these processes is "dominated" or "ruled" by one of the 12 Zodiac signs

Planetary metals were "dominated" or "ruled" by one of the seven planets known by the ancient potion masters. Although they occasionally have a symbol of their own, they were usually symbolized by the planet's symbol. Uranus, Neptune, and Pluto were not yet discovered while potion making was commonly practiced, though many modern potion masters consider them representative of Uranium, Neptunium and Plutonium, respectively.

☞ **Common symbols. Please make sure you use the correct symbol.**

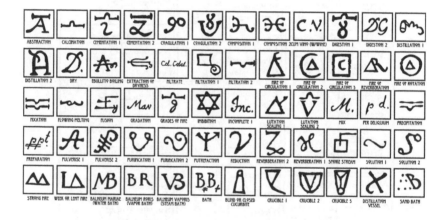

The Six Keys of Eudoxus

☞ THE FIRST KEY

The First Key is that which opens the dark prisons in which the Sulphur is shut up: this is it which knows how to extract the seed out of the body, and which forms the Stone of the philosophers by the conjunction of the spirit with the body -- of sulphur with mercury.

Hermes has manifestly demonstrated the operation of this First Key by these words: In the caverns of the metals there is hidden the Stone, which is venerable, bright in colour, a mind sublime, and an open sea.

This Stone has a bright glittering: it contains a Spirit of a sublime original; it is the Sea of the Wise, in which they angle for their mysterious Fish.

But the operations of the three works have a great deal of analogy one to another, and the philosophers do designedly speak in equivocal terms, to the end that those who have not the Lynx's eyes may pursue wrong, and be lost in this labyrinth, from whence it is very hard to get out. In effect, when one imagines that they speak of one work, they often treat of another.

Take heed, therefore, not to be deceived here; for it is a truth, that in each work the Wise Artist ought to dissolve the body with the spirit; he must cut off the Raven's head, whiten the Black, and vivify the White; yet it is properly in the First operation that the Wise Artist cuts off the head of the Black Dragon and of the Raven.

Hence, Hermes says, What is born of the Crow is the beginning of this Art. Consider that it is by separation of the black, foul, and stinking fume of the Blackest Black that our astral, white, and resplendent Stone is formed, which contains in its veins the blood of the Pelican. It is at this First Purification of the Stone, and at this shining whiteness, that the work of the First Key is ended.

☞ THE SECOND KEY

The Second Key dissolves the compound of the Stone, and begins the separation of the Elements in a philosophical manner: this separation of the elements is not made but by raising up the subtle and pure parts above the thick and terrestrial parts.

He who knows how to sublime the Stone philosophically, justly deserves the name of a philosopher, since he knows the Fire of the Wise, which is the only instrument which can work this sublimation. No philosopher has ever openly revealed this Secret Fire, and this powerful agent, which works all the wonders of the Art: he who shall not understand it, and not know how to distinguish it by the characters whereby it is described, ought to make a stand here, and pray to God to make it clear to him; for the knowledge of this great Secret is rather a gift of Heaven, than a Light acquired by the natural force of reasoning; let him, nevertheless, read the writings of the philosophers; let him meditate; and, above all, let him pray: there is no difficulty which may not in the end be made clear by Work, Meditation, and Prayer.

Without the sublimation of the Stone, the conversion of the Elements and the extraction of the Principles is impossible; and this conversion, which makes Water of Earth, Air of Water, and Fire of Air, is the only way whereby our Mercury can be prepared.

Apply yourself then to know this Secret Fire, which dissolves the Stone naturally and without violence, and makes it dissolve into Water in the great sea of the Wise, by the distillation which is made by the rays of the Sun and Moon.

It is in this manner that the Stone, which, according to Hermes, is the vine of the Wise, becomes their Wine, which, by the operations of Art, produces their rectified Water of Life, and their most sharp Vinegar. The Elements of the Stone cannot be dissolved but by this Nature wholly Divine; nor can a perfect dissolution be made of it, but after a proportioned digestion and putrefaction, at which the operation of the Second Key of the First Work is ended.

☛ THE THIRD KEY

The Third Key comprehends of itself alone a longer train of operations than all the rest together. The philosophers have spoken very little of it, seeing the Perfection of our Mercury depends thereon; the sincerest even, as Artefius, Trevisan, Flammel, have passed in silence the Preparation of our Mercury, and there is hardly one found who has not feigned, instead of showing the longest and the most important of the operations of our Practice. With a design to lend you a hand in this part of the way, which you have to go, and where for want of Light it is impossible to know the true road, I will enlarge myself more than others have done on this Third Key; or at least I will follow in an order, that which they have treated so confusedly, that without the inspiration of Heaven, or without the help of a faithful friend, one remains undoubtedly in this labyrinth, without being able to find a happy deliverance from thence.

I am sure, that you who are the true Sons of Science will receive a very great satisfaction in the explaining of these hidden Mysteries, which regard the separation and the purification of the Principles of our Mercury, which is made by a perfect dissolution and glorification of the body, whence it had its nativity, and by the intimate union of the soul with its body, of whom the Spirit is the only tie which works this conjunction.

This is the Intention, and the essential point of the Operations of this Key, which terminate at the generation of a new substance infinitely nobler than the First.

After the Wise Artist has made a spring of living water come out of the stone, and has pressed out the vine of the philosophers, and has made their wine, he ought to take notice that in this homogeneous substance, which appears under the form of Water, there are three different substances, and three natural principles of bodies -- Salt, Sulphur and Mercury -- which are the spirit, the soul, and the body; and though they appear pure and perfectly united together, there still wants much of their being so; for when by distillation we draw the Water, which is the soul and the spirit, the Body remains in the bottom of the vessel, like a dead, black, and dredgy earth, which, nevertheless, is not to be despised; for in our subject there is nothing which is not good.

The philosopher, John Pontanus, protests that the very superfluities of the Stone are converted into a true essence, and that he who pretends to separate anything from our subject knows nothing of philosophy; for that all which is therein superfluous, unclean, dredgy -- in fine, the whole compound, is made perfect by the action of our Fire.

This advice opens the eyes of those, who, to make an exact purification of the Elements and of the Principles, persuade themselves that they must only take the subtile and cast away the heavy. But Hermes says that power of it is not integral until it be turned into earth; neither ought the sons of science to be ignorant that the Fire and the Sulphur are hidden in the centre of the Earth, and that they must wash it exactly with its spirit, to extract out of it the Fixed Salt, which is the Blood of our Stone. This is the essential Mystery of the operation, which is not accomplished till after a convenient digestion and a slow distillation.

You know that nothing is more contrary than fire and water; but yet the Wise Artist must make peace between the enemies, who radically love each other vehemently. Cosmopolite told the manner thereof in a few words: All things must therefore being purged make Fire and Water to be Friends, which they will easily do in their earth, which had ascended with them. Be then attentive on this point; moisten oftentimes the earth with its water, and you will obtain what you seek. Must not the body be dissolved by the water, and the Earth be penetrated with its Humidity, to be made proper for generation? According to philosophers, the Spirit is Eve, the Body is Adam; they ought to be joined together for the propagation of their species. Hermes says the same in other terms: "For Water is the strongest Nature which surmounts and excites the fixed Nature in the Body, that is, rejoices in it."

In effect, these two substances, which are of the same nature but of different genders, ascend insensibly together, leaving but a little faeces in the bottom of their vessel; so that the soul, spirit, and body, after an exact purification, appear at last inseparably united under a more noble and more perfect Form than it was before, and as different from its first liquid Form as the alcohol of Wine exactly rectified and actuated with its salt is different from the substance of the wine from whence it has been drawn; this comparison is not only very fitting, but it furthermore gives the sons of science a precise knowledge of the operations of the Third Key.

Our Water is a living Spring which comes out of the Stone by a natural miracle of our philosophy. The first of all is the water which issueth out of this Stone. It is Hermes who has pronounced this great Truth. He acknowledges, further, that this water is the foundation of our Art.

The philosophers give it many names; for sometimes they call it wine, sometimes water of life, sometimes vinegar, sometimes oil, according to the different degrees of Preparation, or according to the diverse effects which it is capable of producing.

Yet I let you know that it is properly called the Vinegar of the Wise, and that in the distillation of this Divine Liquor there happens the same thing as in that of common vinegar; you may hence draw instruction: the water and the phlegm ascend first; the oily substance, in which the efficacy of the water consists, comes the last, etc.

It is therefore necessary to dissolve the body entirely to extract all its humidity which contains the precious ferment, the sulphur, that balm of Nature, and wonderful unguent, without which you ought not to hope ever to see in your vessel this blackness so desired by all the philosophers. Reduce then the whole compound into water, and make a perfect union of the volatile with the fixed; it is a precept of Senior's, which deserves attention, that the highest fume should be reduced to the lowest; for the divine water is the thing descending from heaven, the reducer of the soul to its body, which it at length revives.

The Balm of Life is hid in these unclean faeces; you ought to wash them with this celestial water until you have removed away the blackness from them, and then your Water shall be animated with this Fiery Essence, which works all the wonders of our Art.

But, further, that you may not be deceived with the terms of the Compound, I will tell you that the philosophers have two sorts of compounds. The first is the compound of Nature, wherof I have spoken in the First Key; for it is Nature which makes it in a manner incomprehensible to the Artist, who does nothing but lend a hand to Nature by the adhibition of external things, by the means of which she brings forth and produces this admirable compound.

The second is the compound of Art; it is the Wise man who makes it by the secret union of the fixed with the volatile, perfectly conjoined with all prudence, which cannot be acquired but by the lights of a profound philosophy.

The compound of Art is not altogether the same in the Second as in the Third Work; yet it is always the Artist who makes it. Geber defines it, a mixture of Argent vive and Sulphur, that is to say, of the volatile and the fixed; which, acting on one another, are volatilized and fixed reciprocally into a perfect Fixity. Consider the example of Nature; you see that the earth will never produce fruit if it be not penetrated with its humidity, and that the humidity would always remain barren if it were not retained and fixed by the dryness of the earth.

So, in the Art, you can have no success if you do not in the first work purify the Serpent, born of the Slime of the earth; it you do not whiten these foul and black faeces, to separate from thence the white sulphur, which is the Sal Amoniac of the Wise, and their Chaste Diana, who washes herself in the bath; and all this mystery is but the extraction of the fixed salt of our compound, in which the whole energy of our Mercury consists.

The water which ascends by distillation carries up with it a part of this fiery salt, so that the affusion of the water on the body, reiterated many times, impregnates, fattens, and fertilizes our Mercury, and makes it fit to be fixed, which is the end of the second Work. 19. One cannot better explain this Truth than by Hermes, in these words:

When I saw that the water by degrees did become thicker and harder I did rejoice, for I certainly knew that I should find what I sought for.

It is not without reason that the philosophers give this viscous Liquor the name of Pontick Water. Its exuberant ponticity is indeed the true character of its virtue, and the more you shall rectify it, and the more you shall work upon it, the more virtue will it acquire. It has been called the Water of Life, because it gives life to the metals; but it is properly called the great Lunaria, because of its brightness wherewith it shines....

Since I speak only to you, ye true scholars of Hermes, I will reveal to you one secret which you will not find entirely in the books of the philosophers. Some of them say, that of the liquor they make two Mercuries -- the one White and the other Red; Flammel has said more particularly, that one must make use of the citrine Mercury to make the Imbibition of the Red; giving notice to the Sons of Art not to be deceived on this point, as he himself had been, unless the Jew had informed him of the truth.

Others have taught that the White Mercury is the bath of the Moon, and that the Red Mercury is the bath of the Sun. But there are none who have been willing to show distinctly to the Sons of Science by what means they may get these two mercuries. If you apprehend me well, you have the point already cleared up to you.

The Lunaria is the White Mercury, the most sharp Vinegar is the Red Mercury; but the better to determine these two mercuries, feed them with flesh of their own species -- the blood of innocents whose throats are cut; that is to say, the spirits of the bodies are the Bath where the Sun and Moon go to wash themselves.

I have unfolded to you a great mystery, if you reflect well on it; the philosophers who have spoken thereof have passed over this important point very slightly. Cosmopolite has very wittily mentioned it by an ingenious allegory, speaking of the purification of the Mercury: This will be done, says he, if you shall give our old man gold and silver to swallow, that he may consume them, and at length he also dying may be burnt. He makes an end of describing the whole magistery in these terms: Let his ashes be strewed in the water; boil it until it is enough, and you have a medicine to cure the leprosy. You must not be ignorant that Our Old Man is our Mercury; this name indeed agrees with him because He is the first matter of all metals. He is their water, as the same author goes on to say, and to which he gives also the name of steel and of the lodestone; adding for a greater confirmation of what I am about to discover to you, that if gold couples with it eleven times it sends forth its seed, and is debilitated almost unto death; but the Chalybes conceives and begets a son more glorious than the Father.

Behold a great Mystery which I reveal to you without an enigma; this is the secret of the two mercuries which contain the two tinctures. Keep them separately, and do not confound their species, for fear they should beget a monstrous Lineage.

I not only speak to you more intelligibly than any philosopher before has done, but I also reveal to you the most essential point in the Practice; if you meditate thereon, and apply yourself to understand it well; but above all, if you work according to those lights which I give you, you may obtain what you seek for.

And if you come not to these knowledges by the way which I have pointed out to you, I am very well assured that you will hardly arrive at your design by only reading the philosophers. Therefore despair of nothing -- search the source of the Liquor of the Sages, which contains all that is necessary for the work; it is hidden under the Stone -- strike upon it with the Red of Magic Fire, and a clear fountain will issue out; then do as I have shown you, prepare the bath of the King with the blood of the Innocents, and you will have the animated Mercury of the wise, which never loses its virtue, if you keep it in a vessel well closed,

Hermes says, that there is so much sympathy between the purified bodies and the spirits, that they never quit one another when they are united together: because this union resembles that of the soul with the glorified body; after which Faith tells us, there shall be no more separation or death; because the spirits desire to be in the cleansed bodies, and having them, they enliven and dwell in them.

By this you may observe the merit of this precious liquor, to which the philosophers have given more than a thousand different names, which is in sum the great Alcahest, which radically dissolves the metals -- a true permanent water which, after having radically dissolved them, is inseparably united to them, increasing their weight and tincture.

☞ THE FOURTH KEY

The Fourth Key of the Art is the entrance to the Second Work (and a reiteration in part and development of the foregoing): it is this which reduces our Water into Earth; there is but this only Water in the world, which by a bare boiling can be converted into Earth, because the Mercury of the Wise carries in its centre its own Sulphur, which coagulates it. The terrification of the Spirit is the only operation of this work. Boil them with patience; if you have proceeded well, you will not be a long time without perceiving the marks of this coagulation; and if they appear not in their time, they will never appear; because it is an undoubted sign that you have failed in some essential thing in the former operations; for to corporify the Spirit, which is our Mercury, you must have well dissolved the body in which the Sulphur which coagulates the Mercury is enclosed. But Hermes assumes that our mercurial water shall obtain all the virtues which the philosophers attribute to it if it be turned into earth. An earth admirable is it for fertility -- the Land of Promise of the Wise, who, knowing how to make the dew of Heaven fall upon it, cause it to produce fruits of an inestimable price. Cultivate then diligently this precious earth, moisten it often with its own humidity, dry it as often, and you will no less augment its virtue than its weight and its fertility.

☞ THE FIFTH KEY

The Fifth Key includes the Fermentation of the Stone with the perfect body, to make therof the medicine of the Third order. I will say nothing in particular of the operation of the Third work; except that the Perfect Body is a necessary leaven of Our Paste. And that the Spirit ought to make the union of the paste with the leaven in the same manner as water moistens meal, and dissolves the leaven to compose a fermented paste fit to make bread. This comparison is very proper; Hermes first made it, saying, that as a paste cannot be fermented without a ferment; so when you shall have sublimed, cleansed and separated the foulness from the Faeces, and would make the conjunction, put a ferment to them and make the water earth, that the paste may be made a ferment; which repeats the instruction of the whole work, and shows, that just so as the whole lump of the paste becomes leaven, by the action of the ferment which has been added, so all the philosophic confection becomes, by this operation, a leaven proper to ferment a new matter, and to multiply it to infinity. If you observe well how bread is made, you will find the proportions also, which you ought to keep among the matters which compose our philosophical paste. Do not the bakers put more meal than leaven, and more water than the leaven and the meal? The laws of Nature are the rules you ought to follow in the practice of our magistery. I have given you, upon the principal point, all the instructions which are necessary for you, so that it would be superfluous to tell you more of it; particularly concerning the last operations, about which the Adepts have been less reserved than at the First, which are the foundations of the Art.

☞ THE SIXTH KEY

The Sixth Key teaches the Multiplication of the Stone, by the reiteration of the same operation, which consists but in opening and shutting, dissolving and coagulating, imbibing and drying; whereby the virtues of the Stone are infinitely augmentable. As my design has been not to describe entirely the application of the three medicines, but only to instruct you in the more important operations concerning the preparation of Mercury, which the philosophers commonly pass over in silence, to hide the mysteries from the profane which are only intended for the wise, I will tarry no longer on this point, and will tell you nothing more of what relates to the Projection of the Medicine, because the success you expect depends not thereon. I have not given you very full instructions except on the Third Key, because it contains a long train of operations which, though simple and natural, require a great understanding of the Laws of Nature, and of the qualities of Our Matter, as well as a perfect knowledge of chemistry and of the different degrees of heat which are fitting for these operations. I have conducted you by the straight way without any winding; and if you have well minded the road which I have pointed out to you, I am sure that you will go straight to the end without straying. Take this in good part from me, in the design which I had of sparing you a thousand labours and a thousand troubles, which I myself have undergone in this painful journey for want of an assistance such as this is, which I give you from a sincere heart and a tender affection for all the true sons of science. I should much bewail, if, like me, after having known the true matter, you should spend fifteen years entirely in the work, in study and in meditation, without being able to extract out of the Stone the precious juice which it encloses in its bosom, for want of knowing the secret fire of the wise, which makes to run out of this plant (dry and withered in appearance) a water which wets not the hands, and which by a magical union of the dry water of the sea of the wise, is dissolved into a viscous water -- into a mercurial liquor, which is the beginning, the foundation, and the Key of our Art: Convert, separate, and purify the elements, as I have taught you, and you will possess the true Mercury of the philosophers, which will give you the fixed Sulphur and the Universal Medicine. But I give you notice, moreover, that even after you shall be arrived at the knowledge of the Secret Fire of the Wise, yet still you shall not attain your point at your first career. I have erred many years in the way which remains to be gone, to arrive at the mysterious fountain where the King bathes himself, is made young again, and retakes a new life exempt from all sorts of infirmities. Besides this you must know how to purify, to heal, and to animate the royal bath; it is to lend you a hand in this secret way that I have expatiated under the Third Key, where all those operations are described. I wish with all my heart that the instructions which I have given you may enable you to go directly to the End. But remember, ye sons of philosophy, that the knowledge of our Magistery comes rather by the Inspiration of Heaven than from the Lights which we can get by ourselves. This truth is acknowledged by all artists; it is for good reason that it is not enough to work; pray daily, read good books, and meditate night and day on the operations of Nature, and on what she may be able to do when she is assisted by the help of our Art; and by these means you will succeed without doubt in your undertaking. This is all I have now to say to you. I was not willing to make you such a long discourse as the matter seemed to demand; neither have I told you anything but what is essential to our Art; so that if you know the Stone which is the only matter of Our Stone, and if you have the Understanding of Our Fire, which is both secret and natural, you have the Keys of the Art, and you can calcine Our Stone; not by the common calcination which is made by the violence of fire, but by a philosophic calcination which is purely natural. Yet observe this, with the most enlightened philosophers, that there is this difference between the common calcination which is made by the force of Fire and the natural calcination; that the first destroys the body and consumes the greatest part of its radical humidity; but the second does not only preserve the humidity of the body in calcining it, but still considerably augments it. Experience will give you knowledge in the Practice of this great truth, for you will in effect find that this philosophical calcination, which sublimes and distills the Stone in calcining it, much augments its humidity; the reason is that the igneous spirit of the natural fire is corporified in the substances which are analogous to it. Our stone is an Astral Fire which sympathizes with the Natural Fire, and which, as a true Salamander receives it nativity, is nourished and grows in the Elementary Fire, which is geometrically proportioned to it.

The Treasure of Treasures

Nature begets a mineral in the bowels of the earth. There are two kinds of it, which are found in many districts of Europe. The best which has been offered to me, which also has been found genuine in experimentation, is externally in the figure of the greater world, and is in the eastern part of the sphere of the Sun. The other, in the Southern Star, is now in its first efflorescence. The bowels of the earth thrust this forth through its surface. It is found red in its first coagulation, and in it lie hid all the flowers and colours of the minerals. Much has been written about it by the philosophers, for it is of a cold and moist nature, and agrees with the element of water.

So far as relates to the knowledge of it and experiment with it, all the philosophers before me, though they have aimed at it with their missiles, have gone very wide of the mark. They believed that Mercury and Sulphur were the mother of all metals, never even dreaming of making mention meanwhile of a third; and yet when the water is separated from it by Spagyric Art the truth is plainly revealed, though it was unknown to Galen or to Avicenna. But if, for the sake of our excellent physicians, we had to describe only the name, the composition; the dissolution, and coagulation, as in the beginning of the world Nature proceeds with all growing things, a whole year would scarcely suffice me, and, in order to explain these things, not even the skins of numerous cows would be adequate.

Now, I assert that in this mineral are found three principles, which are Mercury, Sulphur, and the Mineral Water which has served to naturally coagulate it. Spagyric science is able to extract this last from its proper juice when it is not altogether matured, in the middle of the autumn, just like a pear from a tree. The tree potentially contains the pear. If the Celestial Stars and Nature agree , the tree first of all puts forth shoots in the month of March; then it thrusts out buds, and when these open the flower appears, and so on in due order until in autumn the pear grows ripe. So is it with the minerals. These are born, in like manner, in the bowels of the earth. Let the Alchemists who are seeking the Treasure of Treasures carefully note this. I will shew them the way, its beginning, its middle, and its end. In the following treatise I will describe the proper Water, the proper Sulphur, and the proper Balm thereof. By means of these three the resolution and composition are coagulated into one.

☛ CONCERNING THE SULPHUR OF CINNABAR

Take mineral Cinnabar and prepare it in the following manner. Cook it with rain water in a stone vessel for three hours. Then purify it carefully, and dissolve it in Aqua Regis, which is composed of equal parts of vitriol, nitre, and sal ammoniac. Another formula is vitriol, saltpetre, alum, and common salt.

Distil this in an alembic. Pour it on again, and separate carefully the pure from the impure thus. Let it putrefy for a month in horse-dung; then separate the elements in the following manner. If it puts forth its signI, commence the distillation by means of an alembic with a fire of the first degree. The water and the air will ascend; the fire and the earth will remain at the bottom. Afterwards join them again, and gradually treat with the ashes. So the water and the air will again ascend first, and afterwards the element of fire, which expert artists recognise. The earth will remain in the bottom of the vessel. This collect there. It is what many seek after and few find.

This dead earth in the reverberatory you will prepare according to the rules of Art, and afterwards add fire of the first degree for five days and nights. When these have elapsed you must apply the second degree for the same number of days and nights, and proceed according to Art with the material enclosed. At length you will find a volatile salt, like a thin alkali, containing in itself the Astrum of fire and earth2. Mix this with the two elements that have been preserved, the water and the earth. Again place it on the ashes for eight days and eight nights, and you will find that which has been neglected by many Artists. Separate this according to your experience, and according to the rules of the Spagyric Art, and you will have a white earth, from which its colour has been extracted. Join the element of fire and salt to the alkalised earth. Digest in a pelican to extract the essence. Then a new earth will be deposited, which put aside.

🖝 CONCERNING THE RED LION

Afterwards take the lion in the pelican which also is found [at] first, when you see its tincture, that is to say, the element of fire which stands above the water, the air, and the earth. Separate it from its deposit by trituration. Thus you will have the true aurum potabile3. Sweeten this with the alcohol of wine poured over it, and then distil in an alembic until you perceive no acidity to remain in the Aqua Regia.

This Oil of the Sun, enclosed in a retort hermetically sealed, you must place for elevation that it may be exalted and doubled in its degree. Then put the vessel, still closely shut, in a cool place. Thus it will not be dissolved, but coagulated. Place it again for elevation and coagulation, and repeat this three times. Thus will be produced the Tincture of the Sun, perfect in its degree. Keep this in its own place.

🖝 CONCERNING THE GREEN LION

Take the vitriol of Venus4, carefully prepared according to the rules of Spagyric Art; and add thereto the elements of water and air which you have reserved. Resolve, and set to putrefy for a month according to instructions. When the putrefaction is finished, you will behold the sign of the elements. Separate, and you will soon see two colours, namely, white and red. The red is above the white. The red tincture of the vitriol is so powerful that it reddens all white bodies, and whitens all red ones, which is wonderful.

Work upon this tincture by means of a retort, and you will perceive a blackness issue forth. Treat it again by means of the retort, repeating the operation until it comes out whitish. Go on, and do not despair of the work. Rectify until you find the true, clear Green Lion, which you will recognise by its great weight. You will see that it is heavy and large. This is the Tincture, transparent gold. You will see marvellous signs of this Green Lion, such as could be bought by no treasures of the Roman Leo. Happy he who has learnt how to find it and use it for a tincture!

This is the true and genuine Balsam5, the Balsam of the Heavenly Stars, suffering no bodies to decay, nor allowing leprosy, gout, or dropsy to take root. It Is given in a dose of one grain, if it has been fermented with Sulphur of Gold.

Ah, Charles the German, where is your treasure? Where are your philosophers? Where your doctors? Where your decocters of woods, who at least purge and relax? Is your heaven reversed? Have your stars wandered out of their course, and are they straying in another orbit, away from the line of limitation, since your eyes are smitten with blindness, as by a carbuncle, and other things making a show of ornament, beauty, and pomp? If your artists only knew that their prince Galen - they call none like him - was sticking in hell, from whence he has sent letters to me, they would make the sign of the cross upon themselves with a fox's tail. In the same way your Avicenna sits in the vestibule of the infernal portal; and I have disputed with him about his aurum potabile, his Tincture of the Philosophers, his Quintessence, and Philosophers' Stone, his Mithridatic, his Theriac, and all the rest. O, you hypocrites, who despise the truths taught you by a true physician, who is himself instructed by Nature, and is a son of God himself! Come, then, and listen, impostors who prevail only by the authority of your high positions! After my death, my disciples will burst forth and drag you to the light, and shall expose your dirty drugs, wherewith up to this time you have compassed the death of princes, and the most invincible magnates of the Christian world. Woe for your necks in the day of judgment! I know that the monarchy will be mine. Mine, too, will be the honour and glory. Not that I praise myself: Nature praises me. Of her I am born; her I follow. She knows me, and I know her. The light which is in her I have beheld in her; outside, too, I have proved the same in the figure of the microcosm, and found it in that universe.

But I must proceed with my design in order to satisfy my disciples to the full extent of their wish. I willingly do this for them, if only skilled in the light of Nature and thoroughly practised in astral matters, they finally become adepts in philosophy, which enables them to know the nature of every kind of water.

Take, then, of this liquid of the minerals which I have described, four parts by weight; of the Earth of red Sol two parts; of Sulphur of Sol one part. Put these together into a pelican, congelate, and dissolve them three times. Thus you will have the Tincture of the Alchemists. We have not here described its weight: but this is given in the book on Transmutations6.

So, now, he who has one to a thousand ounces of the Astrum Solis shall also tinge his own body of Sol.

If you have the Astrum of Mercury, in the same manner, you will tinge the whole body of common Mercury. If you have the Astrum of Venus you will, in like manner, tinge the whole body of Venus, and change it into the best metal. These facts have all been proved. The same must also be understood as to the Astra of the other planets, as Saturn, Jupiter, Mars, Luna, and the rest. For tinctures are also prepared from these: concerning which we now make no mention in this place, because we have already dwelt at sufficient length upon them in the book on the Nature of Things and in the Archidoxies. So, too, the first entity of metals and terrestrial minerals have been made, sufficiently clear for Alchemists to enable them to get the Alchemists' Tincture.

This work, the Tincture of the Alchemists, need not be one of nine months; but quickly, and without any delay, you may go on by the Spaygric Art of the Alchemists, and, in the space of forty days, you can fix this alchemical substance, exalt it, putrefy it, ferment it, coagulate it into a stone, and produce the Alchemical Phoenix7. But it should be noted well that the Sulphur of Cinnabar becomes the Flying Eagle, whose wings fly away without wind, and carry the body of the phoenix to the nest of the parent, where it is nourished by the element of fire, and the young ones dig out its eyes: from whence there emerges a whiteness, divided in its sphere, into a sphere and life out of its own heart, by the balsam of its inward parts, according to the property of the cabalists.

Hunting the Blacke Toade

The study of alchemical symbolism is in many respects similar to that of Christian symbolism in works of art and literature. The major difference, however, is that the key to the latter is well known while the key to alchemy has been lost. Its re-discovery is not a matter of a single insight but rather of a meticulous and long-lasting comparative study of surviving texts and iconography. It is now fairly obvious that there were several "schools" of symbolism within European alchemy, sometimes overlapping, sometimes borrowing individual symbols from other systems, or even distorting the ideas of earlier writers. These schools should be clearly defined along with the kind of symbols used by them. Even though such "perfect" definitions may not reflect any actual alchemical works, it would be very useful for reference in any future studies, as well as for the analysis of chronological and geographical spreading of alchemical ideas. Some of such widely defined groups of symbolism and differences between them can be easily seen but have not been properly described yet.

Many scholars stress the fact that most alchemical notions, such as the Philosophers' Stone or the Materia Prima, are denoted by a wide range of names and symbols, and give long lists of examples. But a really helpful kind of "alchemical dictionary" would be to analyze particular clearly defined symbols as used by different alchemical authors and find out their various meanings. A full study of this kind is obviously beyond the possibilities of any individual researcher so I decided to make a small beginning by an attempt to clarify the symbol of the Toad. I chose it because it is not as common as the Lion or the Eagle, and therefore requires less research, but at the same time it is quite distinct and well defined.

Any symbol appearing in an alchemical treatise should be studied from two points of view:

1) Its meaning in other symbolic systems of the period or earlier.

2) Its context in different alchemical treatises.

In the first case care must be taken not to refer to symbolism of the ancient Egyptians or Chinese, as over-enthusiastic occultists tend to do, but rather stick to medieval and renaissance Europe, with possible classical symbols that may have been known there. In the second case the special points to note would be the frequency (and therefore importance) of the symbol in question, whether it appears at the beginning or at the end of the process described, whether it is in a group of three, four, seven, or some other number of symbols, etc.

One of the earliest appearances of the Toad symbol in alchemical literature and iconography seems to be that in the works of George Ripley, in which it plays a very prominent, or even central, part. His short poem The Vision describes an alchemical process veiled in symbols. The Toad first drinks "juice of Grapes" until it is so filled up that "casts it Venom" and "begins to swell" as a result of poisoning. Then the Toad dies in its "Cave" and the usual sequence of colour changes follows: black, various colours, white and red. Thus the Venom is changed into powerful Medicine.

The famous Ripley Scrowle has not been available to me in its entirety but from several published fragments it seems that it presents a similar, though considerably extended, process of the Toad undergoing various chemical changes. It reappears in various points of this symbolic road, clearly suggesting continuity. In some versions the Toad is also the final symbol of the Philosophers' Stone.

It would, therefore, appear that the Toad is here used as the symbol of the First Matter of the Great Work (as different from the cosmological Prima Materia), which is worked upon until the Stone is obtained. The symbolic sense of choosing this symbol finds confirmation in the fact that toad was believed by Ripley's contemporaries to be a venomous animal, highly repugnant, but containing a stone of great value in its head. That stone has the power of curing bites and is an antidote against poison. This common belief found its way to Shakespeare's As You Like It:

Sweet are the uses of adversity;
Which like the toad, ugly and venomous,
Wears yet a precious jewel in his head.

Another English author wrote in 1569: "There is to be found in the heads of old and great toads a stone they call borax or stelon, which being used in a ring gives a forewarning against venom".

Eirenaeus Philalethes in his comentary to Ripley's Vision says that the Toad symbolizes gold. This view may have been influenced by Michael Sendivogius's statement that the Philosophers' Stone is nothing else but "gold digested to the highest degree", especially as Philalethes was his admirer and adopted his pseudonym of Cosmopolita.

As we do not know the First Matter of Ripley, it is difficult to say whether Eirenaeus Philalethes is right. Ripley himself in his most famous work The Twelve Gates, which is less symbolic and uses early chemical terminology, remarks in the first Gate (Calcination):

> The head of the crow that token call we,
> and some men call it the crow's bill.
> Some call it the ashes of Hermes tree,
> Our toad of the earth that eateth his fill,
> and thus they name after their will.
> Some name it by which it is mortificate,
> The spirit of the earth with venom intoxicate.

The Toad is therefore clearly identified here as the stage of Nigredo or Raven's Head, but also connected with earth. Interestingly in the nineth Gate (Fermentation, which is the same as Digestion) Ripley says:

> Earth is gold, and so is the soul also,
> Not common gold, but ours thus elementate.

It is, therefore, clear that in Ripley's works the Toad symbolized the First Matter of the Great Work that was obtained in its first stage of Calcination or Nigredo. It may be gold but then the choice of the symbol would appear strange - it should rather be something base and vulgar. It is often said of the First Matter that it can be found everywhere but fools cannot see it, and this opinion would fit the Toad symbol much better. For instance, the anonymous author of the poem Hunting the Greene Lyon says:

And choose what thou shalt finde of meanest price:

> Leave sophisters, and following my advice,
> Be not deluded; for the truth is one,

'Tis not in many things, this is Our Stone:

> At first appearing in a garb defiled,
> And, to deal plainly, it is Saturn's childe.
> His price is meane, his venom very great
> His constitution cold, devoid of heat.

This aspect of the toad symbol in medieval imagery is also stressed by the medieval writer Catelanus when he says that unicorns live in caves "amid toads and other noxious, loathy reptiles".

The Toad as a symbol of only one phase in the alchemical process appears also in another poem by Ripley:

> The showers cease, the dews, which fell
> For six weeks, do not rise;
> The ugly toad, that did so swell,
> With swelling, bursts and dies.

This is clearly the same chemical process as in his Vision, where almost exactly the same words are used:

> A Toad full Ruddy I saw, did drink the juice of Grapes so fast,
> Till over-charged with the broth, his Bowels all to brast:
> And after that, from poyson'd Bulk he cast his Venom fell,
> For Grief and Pain whereof his Members all began to swell.

Another of the early English alchemists, Bloomfield, in his Camp of Philosophy lists the Toad as one of the names of the Elixir or Philosophers' Stone itself:

Our great Elixir most high of price,
Our Azot, our Basiliske, and our Adrop, our Cocatrice.
Some call it also a substance exuberate,
Some call it Mercury of metalline essence,
Some limus deserti from his body evacuate,
Some the Eagle flying fro' the north with violence,
Some call It a Toade for his great vehemence,
But few or none at all doe name it in its kinde,
It is a privy quintessence; keep it well in minde.

Mary Anne Atwood interprets all these names as reflecting the Stone on various stages of the Great Work: "being sublimed at first, it is called a serpent, dragon, or green lion, on account of its strength and crude vitality, which putrefying, becomes a stronger poison, and their venomous toad; which afterwards appearing calcined by its proper fire, is called magnesia and lead of the wise".

It can be summed up, therefore, that in the English alchemical tradition the Toad is a symbol of the First Matter of the Work, which is Saturnine in nature (which does not have to mean lead but any substance associated with Saturn). Sometimes it refers only the the phase of Putrefaction or Caput Corvi, on account of its Saturnine symbolism ("Regnum Saturni"), sometimes also to the Philosophers' Stone itself, as the "jewel" hidden in the Toad's head (i.e. in the First Matter). This kind of symbolism seems to have been continued by later alchemists in England, through continuous interest in the works of Ripley displayed by such authors as Elias Ashmole, Eirenaeus Philalates, or Samuel Norton, the grandchild of Ripley's supposed apprentice Thomas Norton.

One of the interesting tree diagrams in Norton's Mercurius Redivivus presents the Toad at the roots of the Tree of the Great Work, with two lions at its sides. The Toad reaches for the Grapes above it, thus clearly refering to Ripley's imagery from his Vision.

The well known illustration from Ashmole's Theatrum Chemicum Britannicum shows the Toad at the bottom of the symbolic process, probably indicating its beginning. It is interesting that it joins the male and female figures, as if it symbolized the power of attraction with some sexual overtones. The whole figure is entitled "Spiritus, Anima, Corpus", of which the Corpus or Body is the male-female pair. The whole possible sexual aspect of alchemy is still completely unknown and waiting to be explained but it may be interesting to note that Thomas Vaughan, who illustrated Ashmole's collection, made numerous sexual references in his own alchemical works, especially Aula Lucis. In his notebooks Vaughan explained how he had made the "oil of Halcali" with the help of his wife. According to A.E. Waite this oil is the First Matter which connects it with our Toad symbol.

The sexual symbolism of the Toad can also be found outside alchemy, which strengthens our argument. On the great painting of Hieronymus Bosch The Garden of Earthly Delights, on its right wing, there is a figure of a woman with a toad on her breast which symbolizes the sin of debauchery. A sculpture in Strasbourg entitled The Seducer of Unfaithful Virgins depicts snakes and toads climbing up a handsome youth's back while he holds forth an apple. So the toad may be understood to symbolize the power of sexual instinct, the force of attraction of the opposites, which in the official morality was seen as something loathsome and vulgar.

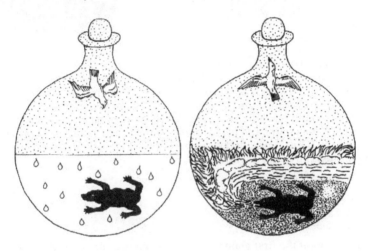

A work that would seem to spring from a totally different tradition, The Crowning of Nature, uses the Toad symbol in two of the 67 figures. These are numbers 17 Fermentation and 18 Separation of the Elements. The text accompanying the pictures, however, strongly resembles the Ripleyan ideas: "But by the Toad, here understand the sphere of Saturn swelling with tincture, or his heaven to be great and impregnate therewith, and by and by ready to bring forth, which by the ejection of the four elements appears most plainly in the next Chapter." The Saturnine nature of the First Matter (or Chemical Subject, as it is called here) is confirmed in figure 2 and its text, which agrees with our conclusion reached above. Ripley's "casting of Venom" by the Toad is paralleled here in figure 18. In both cases the White Dove is above the Toad, probably signifying the volatile nature of the "tincture" or Ripley's Juice of Grapes.

The 18th century published version of the series (without text) produced by Johann Conrad Barchusen has some additional figures, extending the set to 78. Plate I also utilizes the Toad symbol in connection with those of the Pelican, the Lion, and the Salamander, surrounding the Mercury of the Philosophers. Adam McLean interprets the whole as representing the four elements but it is not quite obvious, as the bird at the top is clearly the Pelican, usually not a symbol of the Air. It is also difficult to see any  obvious connection of the Lion with the Water. It is true that there are the standard triangle symbols of two of the elements beside the Lion and the Toad but in that case the symbolism of this plate would not be uniform with the symbolism of the whole series and would have to be treated as a later addition. On the other hand the creatures can be seen as representing the phases of the Great Work. In the original Crowning of Nature these are found in the following series of plates:

    Green Lion   7-8
    Toad   17-18
    Pelican   37
    Salamander   41-55 and 58
    Angel/Stone 66-67

Seen in this light the first plate from Barchusen is a summary of the whole process of the Great Work and thus an integral part of the series. The only objection may be that the very important symbol of the Dove appearing on plates 10-36 is not included. It seems, however, (and is supported by the accompanying text) that the Dove is only the indication of the direction in which the Spirit (or the volatile principle) goes at any stage.

 Of the 17th century Rosicrucian heirs to the alchemical tradition I found only two who used the Toad symbol. The less important in this context is Johann Daniel Mylius. In the very numerous engravings found in his works the Toad appears only on the title page of Opus Medico-Chymicum, inside the triangle of Air, chained to the Eagle above it. It probably refers to the volatile (and therefore "aerial") principle of solid bodies or, otherwise, to "fixing of the volatile". It is interesting that the same image of "bird above toad" appeared in The Crowning of Nature but without the chain joining them. In the text of the latter, however, mention is made about fixing the Elements cast forth by the Toad until they are inseparable. Some shift of meaning must have occured between the two uses of this kind of symbolism.

The most striking thing, however, is that Michael Maier has exactly the same symbol in one half of his personal coat-of-arms as displayed on his portrait in Atalanta Fugiens, and that he used it also as the main symbolic emblem of Avicenna in Symbola Aureae Mensae where it is clearly explained as Fixing the Volatile.

Maier used the Toad symbol in a different context again in Atalanta Fugiens in emblem 5, where it is placed by a man on a woman's breast. The epigram to this emblem is in many ways similar to Ripley's Vision:

> To woman's breast apply the chilly toad,
> So that it drinks her milk, just like a child.
> Then let it swell into a massive growth,
> And let the woman sicken, and then die.
> You make from this a noble medicine,
> Which drives the poison from the human heart.

In this case the Toad drinks Virgin's Milk instead of Juice of Grapes, which may be just different terminology. However, it is the woman who dies, not the Toad. The sexual interpretation can also have been intended as a woman with a toad on her breast is identical with the symbol of debauchery or sexual attraction used by Bosch.

The above cases of Toad symbolism in alchemy are probably very incomplete but even on this basis it can be concluded that there definitely is some continuity in its used from the 15th to the 17th centuries, although occassional shifts in meaning are also noticeable. These may possibly be due to the simultaneous shift from physical alchemy of Ripley and his contemporaries (i.e. probably describing actual chemical processes) to the highly spiritualized (and possibly incorporating the sexual aspect) alchemy of the 17th century Rosicrucian Englightenment.

Plants Containing
Planetary Metals

☛ LEAD

1. Nyssa sylvatica MARSHALL - Black Gum (Leaf) 0.2-182 ppm

2. Symphoricarpos orbiculatus MOENCH. - Buckbush (Stem) 2-176 ppm

3. Juniperus virginiana L. - Red Cedar (Shoot) 0.7-132 ppm

4. Nyssa sylvatica MARSHALL - Black Gum (Stem) 0.1-132 ppm

5. Prunus serotina EHRH. - Black Cherry (Stem) 0.2-108 ppm

6. Carya glabra (MILLER) SWEET - Pignut Hickory (Shoot) 2-103 ppm

7. Rhus copallina L. - Dwarf Sumac (Stem) 0.2-92 ppm

8. Fucus vesiculosus L. - Bladderwrack (Plant) 91 ppm

9. Diospyros virginiana L. - American Persimmon (Stem) 0.2-81 ppm

10. Quercus alba L. - White Oak (Stem) 0.2-76 ppm

11. Prunus serotina EHRH. - Black Cherry (Leaf) 0.3-67 ppm

12. Rhus copallina L. - Dwarf Sumac (Leaf) 0.2-67 ppm

13. Malus domestica BORKH. - Apple (Fruit) 0.002-64 ppm

14. Pinus echinata MILLER - Shortleaf Pine (Shoot) 1.7-63 ppm

15. Lycopersicon esculentum MILLER - Tomato (Fruit) 0.003-60 ppm

16. Quercus stellata WANGENH. - Post Oak (Stem) 0.7-59 ppm

17. Liquidambar styraciflua L. - American Styrax (Stem) 0.2-57 ppm

18. Carya ovata (MILL.) K. KOCH - Shagbark Hickory (Shoot) 0.7-46 ppm

19. Sassafras albidum (NUTT.) NEES - Sassafras (Stem) 0.1-37 ppm

20. Diospyros virginiana L. - American Persimmon (Leaf) 0.5-35 ppm

21. Sassafras albidum (NUTT.) NEES - Sassafras (Leaf) 1-34 ppm

22. Quercus velutina LAM. - Black Oak (Stem) 1.5-31 ppm

23. Asparagus officinalis L. - Asparagus (Shoot) 1.5-30 ppm

24. Liquidambar styraciflua L. - American Styrax (Leaf) 0.4-25 ppm

25. Quercus phellos L. - Willow Oak (Stem) 0.4-21 ppm

26. Rhus glabra L. - Smooth Sumac (Stem) 0.4-20 ppm

27. Hypericum perforatum L. - Common St. Johnswort (Leaf) 6-18 ppm

28. Quercus rubra L. - Northern Red Oak (Stem) 1.4-17 ppm

29. Zea mays L. - Corn (Seed) 0-14 ppm

30. Hypericum perforatum L. - Common St. Johnswort (Plant) 2-12 ppm

31. Prunus domestica L. - Plum (Fruit) 0.02-11.9 ppm

32. Phaseolus vulgaris L. - Blackbean (Fruit) 0.01-10.5 ppm

33. Cinnamomum sieboldii - Japanese Cinnamon (Root Bark) 9 ppm

34. Vitis vinifera L. - Grape (Fruit) 0.02-9 ppm

35. Vigna unguiculata (L.) WALP. - Cowpea (Seed) 0.4-8.4 ppm

36. Cinnamomum sieboldii - Japanese Cinnamon (Bark) 8 ppm

37. Citrus paradisi MacFAD. - Grapefruit (Fruit) 0.02-7.7 ppm

38. Lactuca sativa L. - Lettuce (Leaf) 0.02-6 ppm

39. Urtica dioica L. - European Nettle (Leaf) 1-6 ppm

40. Brassica oleracea L. var. capitata L. - Cabbage (Leaf) 0.002-5.8 ppm

☞ TIN

1. Schisandra chinensis (TURCZ.) BAILL. - Chinese Magnoliavine (Fruit) 940 ppm

2. Elytrigia repens (L.) NEVSKI - Couchgrass (Plant) 67 ppm

3. Juniperus communis L. - Common Juniper (Fruit) 63 ppm

4. Silybum marianum (L.) GAERTN. - Milk Thistle (Plant) 42 ppm

5. Gentiana lutea L. - Yellow Gentian (Root) 40 ppm

6. Cypripedium pubescens WILLD. - Ladyslipper (Root) 33 ppm

7. Rhodymenia palmata - Dulse (Plant) 33 ppm

8. Althaea officinalis L. - Marshmallow (Root) 29 ppm

9. Valeriana officinalis L. - Valerian (Root) 28 ppm

10. Chondrus crispus (L.) STACKH. - Irish Moss (Plant) 27 ppm

11. Urtica dioica L. - European Nettle (Leaf) 27 ppm

12. Achillea millefolium L. - Yarrow (Plant) 26 ppm

13. Berberis vulgaris L. - Barberry (Root) 26 ppm

14. Cnicus benedictus L. - Blessed Thistle (Plant) 25 ppm

15. Trifolium pratense L. - Red Clover (Flower) 25 ppm

16. Fucus vesiculosus L. - Bladderwrack (Plant) 24 ppm

17. Glycyrrhiza glabra L. - Licorice (Root) 24 ppm

18. Harpagophytum procumbens DC. - Devil's Claw (Root) 24 ppm

19. Mentha pulegium L. - European Pennyroyal (Plant) 24 ppm

20. Rumex crispus L. - Curly Dock (Root) 24 ppm

21. Cucurbita pepo L. - Pumpkin (Seed) 23 ppm

22. Humulus lupulus L. - Hops (Fruit) 22 ppm

23. Myrica cerifera L. - Bayberry (Bark) 22 ppm

24. Rosa canina L. - Rose (Fruit) 22 ppm

25. Arctium lappa L. - Gobo (Root) 21 ppm

26. Caulophyllum thalictroides (L.) MICHX. - Blue Cohosh (Root) 21 ppm

27. Chrysanthemum parthenium (L.) BERNH. - Feverfew (Plant) 21 ppm

28. Plantago psyllium L. - Psyllium (Seed) 21 ppm

29. Ruscus aculeatus L. - Butcher's Broom (Root) 21 ppm

30. Dioscorea sp. - Wild Yam (Root) 19 ppm

31. Smilax spp - Sarsaparilla (Root) 18 ppm

32. Viburnum opulus L. - Crampbark (Bark) 18 ppm

33. Viscum album L. - European Mistletoe (Leaf) 18 ppm

34. Echinacea spp - Coneflower (Root) 17 ppm

35. Thymus vulgaris L. - Common Thyme (Leaf) 17 ppm

36. Panax ginseng C. MEYER - Chinese Ginseng (Root) 16 ppm

37. Ulmus rubra MUHLENB. - Slippery Elm (Bark) 16 ppm

38. Stevia rebaudiana (BERT.) HEMSL. - Ca-A-E (Leaf) 15 ppm

39. Equisetum arvense L. - Field Horsetail (Plant) 14 ppm

40. Larrea tridentata (SESSE & MOC. ex DC.) COV. - Chaparral (Plant) 14 ppm

41. Crataegus oxycantha L. - Hawthorn (Fruit) 13 ppm

42. Polygonum multiflorum THUNB. - Chinese Cornbind (Root) 13 ppm

43. Taraxacum officinale WIGG. - Dandelion (Root) 13 ppm

44. Zingiber officinale ROSCOE - Ginger (Rhizome) 13 ppm

45. Centella asiatica (L.) URBAN - Gotu Kola (Leaf) 12 ppm

46. Hordeum vulgare L. - Barley (Stem) 12 ppm

47. Juglans nigra L. - Black Walnut (Fruit) 12 ppm

48. Salix alba L. - White Willow (Bark) 12 ppm

49. Verbascum thapsus L. - Mullein (Leaf) 12 ppm

50. Vitis vinifera L. - Grape (Stem) 12 ppm

51. Agathosma betulina (BERGIUS) PILL. - Buchu (Leaf) 11 ppm

52. Aloe vera (L.) BURM. f. - Bitter Aloes (Leaf) 11 ppm

53. Barosma betulina (BERG.) BARTL. & WENDL. f. - Buchu (Leaf) 11 ppm

54. Ephedra sinica STAPF - Ma Huang (Plant) 11 ppm

55. Foeniculum vulgare MILLER - Fennel (Fruit) 11 ppm

56. Hydrangea arborescens L. - Smooth Hydrangea (Root) 11 ppm

57. Mentha x piperita L. - Peppermint (Leaf) 11 ppm

58. Nepeta cataria L. - Catnip (Plant) 11 ppm

59. Turnera diffusa WILLD. - Damiana (Leaf) 11 ppm

60. Carthamus tinctorius L. - Safflower (Flower) 10 ppm

61. Chamaemelum nobile (L.) ALL. - Garden Camomile (Flower) 10 ppm

62. Hibiscus sabdariffa L. - Roselle (Flower) 10 ppm

63. Prunus persica (L.) BATSCH - Peach (Bark) 9.4 ppm

64. Hydrastis canadensis L. - Goldenseal (Root) 9.3 ppm

65. Euphrasia officinalis L. - Eyebright (Plant) 8 ppm

66. Salvia officinalis L. - Sage (Leaf) 8 ppm

67. Yucca baccata TORR. - Spanish Bayonet (Root) 8 ppm

68. Cymbopogon citratus (DC. ex NEES) STAPF - West Indian Lemongrass (Plant) 7.1 ppm

69. Lobelia inflata L. - Indian Tobacco (Leaf) 7 ppm

70. Symphytum officinale L. - Comfrey (Root) 6.7 ppm

71. Allium sativum L. - Garlic (Bulb) 6 ppm

72. Avena sativa L. - Oats (Plant) 6 ppm

73. Rhamnus purshianus DC. - Cascara Sagrada (Bark) 5.1 ppm

74. Capsicum annuum L. - Bell Pepper (Fruit) 5 ppm

75. Angelica sinensis (OLIV.) DIELS - Dang Gui (Root) 4 ppm

76. Trigonella foenum-graecum L. - Fenugreek (Seed) 4 ppm

77. Tabebuia heptaphylla (VELL.) TOLEDO - Pau D'Arco (Bark) 3.7 ppm

78. Bertholletia excelsa HUMB. & BONPL. - Brazilnut (Seed) 3.5 ppm

79. Citrus paradisi MacFAD. - Grapefruit (Fruit) 0.66-3.3 ppm

80. Carya ovata (MILL.) K. KOCH - Shagbark Hickory (Seed) 3.2 ppm

81. Daucus carota L. - Carrot (Root) 0-3 ppm

82. Beta vulgaris L. - Beet (Root) 0.8-2.8 ppm

83. Corylus avellana L. - English Filbert (Seed) 2.7 ppm

84. Symphoricarpos orbiculatus MOENCH. - Buckbush (Stem) 0.5-2.6 ppm

85. Quercus alba L. - White Oak (Bark) 2.2 ppm

86. Carya illinoensis (WANGENH.) K. KOCH - Pecan (Seed) 1.8 ppm

87. Zea mays L. - Corn (Seed) 1-1.8 ppm

88. Juglans nigra L. - Black Walnut (Seed) 1.7 ppm

89. Cocos nucifera L. - Coconut (Seed) 1.5 ppm

90. Scutellaria lateriflora L. - Maddog Skullcap (Plant) 1.2 ppm

☞ IRON

1. Taraxacum officinale WIGG. - Dandelion (Leaf) 500-5,000 ppm

2. Echinacea spp - Coneflower (Root) 700-4,800 ppm

3. Symphoricarpos orbiculatus MOENCH. - Buckbush (Stem) 19-4,400 ppm

4. Valerianella locusta (L.) LATERRADE - Corn Salad (Plant) 3,519-4,143 ppm

5. Artemisia vulgaris L. - Mugwort (Plant) 1,200-3,900 ppm

6. Boehmeria nivea (L.) GAUDICH. - Ramie (Plant) 1,500-3,500 ppm

7. Physalis ixocarpa BROT. - Tomatillo (Fruit) 14-2,974 ppm

8. Harpagophytum procumbens DC. - Devil's Claw (Root) 2,900 ppm

9. Asiasarum heterotropoides MAEK. - Asian Wild Ginger (Root) 450-2,800 ppm

10. Asiasarum sieboldii (MIQ.) MAEK. - Siebold's Wild Ginger (Root) 450-2,800 ppm

11. Stellaria media (L.) VILLARS - Chickweed (Plant) 2,530 ppm

12. Verbascum thapsus L. - Mullein (Leaf) 2,360 ppm

13. Mentha pulegium L. - European Pennyroyal (Plant) 2,310 ppm

14. Carthamus tinctorius L. - Safflower (Flower) 81-2,200 ppm

15. Petasites japonicus (SIEBOLD & ZUCC.) MAXIM. - Butterbur (Plant) 2,000-2,100 ppm

16. Amaranthus spinosus L. - Spiny pigweed (Leaf) 22-1,965 ppm

17. Polystichum polyblepharum (ROEM.) PRESL - Chinese Polystichum (Plant) 500-1,900 ppm

18. Trifolium pratense L. - Red Clover (Shoot) 10-1,850 ppm

19. Nyssa sylvatica MARSHALL - Black Gum (Leaf) 8-1,820 ppm

20. Angelica dahurica BENTH & HOOK. - Bai Zhi (Root) 1,800 ppm

21. Schizonepeta tenuifolia BRIQ. - Ching-Chieh (Plant) 1,700 ppm

22. Caulophyllum thalictroides (L.) MICHX. - Blue Cohosh (Root) 1,640ppm

23. Ruscus aculeatus L. - Butcher's Broom (Root) 1,640 ppm

24. Diospyros virginiana L. - American Persimmon (Stem) 3-1,620 ppm

25. Amaranthus sp. - Pigweed (Leaf) 23-1,527 ppm

26. Thymus vulgaris L. - Common Thyme (Plant) 1,075-1,508 ppm

27. Camellia sinensis (L.) KUNTZE - Tea (Leaf) 189-1,500 ppm

28. Manihot esculenta CRANTZ - Cassava (Leaf) 28-1,500 ppm

29. Arctium lappa L. - Gobo (Root) 8-1,470 ppm

30. Prunus serotina EHRH. - Black Cherry (Leaf) 20-1,440 ppm

31. Berberis vulgaris L. - Barberry (Root) 1,410 ppm

32. Anemarrhena asphodeloides BUNGE - Chih-Mu (Rhizome) 90-1,400 ppm

33. Peucedanum decursivum (MIQ.) MAX. - Qian Hu (Plant) 780-1,400 ppm

34. Nepeta cataria L. - Catnip (Plant) 1,380 ppm

35. Chamissoa altissima (JACQ.) HBK - Guanique (Leaf) 137-1,370 ppm

36. Cynanchum atratum BUNGE - Bai-Wei (Root) 1,350 ppm

37. Juniperus virginiana L. - Red Cedar (Shoot) 11-1,320 ppm

38. Polygonum cuspidatum SIEBOLD & ZUCC. - Japanese Knotweed (Plant) 360-1,300 ppm

39. Senna occidentalis (L.) H. IRWIN & BARNEBY - Coffee Senna (Seed) 1,300 ppm

40. Equisetum arvense L. - Field Horsetail (Plant) 698-1,230 ppm

☞ COPPER

1. Prunus serotina EHRH. - Black Cherry (Stem) 1.3-378 ppm
2. Liquidambar styraciflua L. - American Styrax (Stem) 0.6-360 ppm
3. Nyssa sylvatica MARSHALL - Black Gum (Leaf) 1.25-182 ppm
4. Liquidambar styraciflua L. - American Styrax (Leaf) 2.8-164 ppm
5. Symphoricarpos orbiculatus MOENCH. - Buckbush (Stem) 3.8-132 ppm
6. Diospyros virginiana L. - American Persimmon (Stem) 0.2-108 ppm
7. Sassafras albidum (NUTT.) NEES - Sassafras (Leaf) 1.6-102 ppm
8. Lycopersicon esculentum MILLER - Tomato (Fruit) 0.4-100 ppm
9. Brassica oleracea L. var. capitata L. - Cabbage (Leaf) 0.3-87 ppm
10. Corylus avellana L. - English Filbert (Seed) 13-82 ppm
11. Sassafras albidum (NUTT.) NEES - Sassafras (Stem) 0.2-56 ppm
12. Sesamum indicum L. - Sesame (Plant) 14-56 ppm
13. Carya glabra (MILLER) SWEET - Pignut Hickory (Shoot) 0.9-55 ppm
14. Brassica oleracea L. var. botrytis L. - Broccoli (Leaf) 0.68-52 ppm
15. Carya ovata (MILL.) K. KOCH - Shagbark Hickory (Shoot) 1.25-45 ppm
16. Phaseolus vulgaris L. - Blackbean (Fruit) 0.62-45 ppm
17. Brassica oleracea L. - Collards (Leaf) 2-43 ppm
18. Cucumis sativus L. - Cucumber (Fruit) 0.3-42 ppm
19. Quercus stellata WANGENH. - Post Oak (Stem) 1.2-42 ppm
20. Anacardium occidentale L. - Cashew (Seed) 22-37 ppm
21. Rosa canina L. - Rose (Fruit) 1.8-36 ppm
22. Eupatorium odoratum L. - Jack na bush (Leaf) 35 ppm
23. Rhizophora mangle L. - Red Mangrove (Leaf) 35 ppm
24. Prunus domestica L. - Plum (Fruit) 0.33-34 ppm
25. Cocos nucifera L. - Coconut (Seed) 3.2-33 ppm
26. Pistacia vera L. - Pistachio (Seed) 11-33 ppm
27. Psophocarpus tetragonolobus (L.) DC. - Asparagus Pea (Seed) 28-33 ppm
28. Senna obtusifolia (L.) H.IRWIN & BARNEBY - Sicklepod (Seed) 9-32 ppm
29. Nyssa sylvatica MARSHALL - Black Gum (Stem) 0.3-31 ppm
30. Quercus velutina LAM. - Black Oak (Stem) 1.5-31 ppm
31. Cucurbita maxima DUCH. - Pumpkin (Leaf) 4.2-30 ppm
32. Helianthus tuberosus L. - Jerusalem Artichoke (Plant) 8-30 ppm
33. Momordica charantia L. - Bitter Melon (Fruit) 30 ppm
34. Prunus persica (L.) BATSCH - Peach (Fruit) 0.3-30 ppm
35. Rhus copallina L. - Dwarf Sumac (Stem) 1.8-30 ppm

36. Rumex acetosa L. - Garden Sorrel (Leaf) 3-30 ppm

37. Arctium lappa L. - Gobo (Root) 29 ppm

38. Lactuca sativa L. - Lettuce (Leaf) 0.36-29 ppm

39. Prunus serotina EHRH. - Black Cherry (Leaf) 0.8-29 ppm

40. Quercus phellos L. - Willow Oak (Stem) 1-29 ppm

☞ MERCURY

1. Cinnamomum aromaticum NEES - Cassia (Plant) 60 ppm

2. Fucus vesiculosus L. - Bladderwrack (Plant) 40 ppm

3. Rhodymenia palmata - Dulse (Plant) 26 ppm

4. Lycium chinense MILL. - Wolfberry (Fruit) 8 ppm

5. Chondrus crispus (L.) STACKH. - Irish Moss (Plant) 7 ppm

6. Juncus effusus L. - Rush (Pith) 1.41 ppm

7. Arctium lappa L. - Gobo (Root) 1.27 ppm

☞ SILVER

1. Lycopersicon esculentum MILLER - Tomato (Fruit) 0-1.4 ppm

2. Quercus rubra L. - Northern Red Oak (Stem) 0-1.32 ppm

Alphabetical Index
of Potions

Acknowledgments

The authors of this book, as well as Mythos Books publishing would like to thank everyone who contributed in any way whatsoever to this text.

We would especially like to thank Mrs. J. for her exceptional prowess in conjuring — and "adulterantes verbum" — without which none of this publication would have been even remotely possible.

Gratitude also goes to Messrs. Harry and Albert Wonskolaser whose combined skills of production lent themselves to clarity and direction in the layout and formatting of "Advanced Potion Making."

There can be no publicizing of this book without mentioning Mr. A. Sidney Patrick Rickman who's craft is known in more than merely the world of wizarding education for excellence which we all aspire to.

Last, but certainly not least, we would like to thank Potions Master N. Green, Potions Master T. O'Dell, Professor Goodrick, Professor A. Percival Arnold, Professor Orr and all the wizards and witches who, through many ages of trial and error, have refined and perfected the potions listed herein.

If we have missed anyone we also thank you truly and sincerely. Our hope is this text will find a loving home in the hands of at least one student who can work its magic, improve on its instruction, and carry its contents throughout their life.

CPSIA information can be obtained
at www.ICGtesting.com
Printed in the USA
LVHW030503120720
660228LV00006B/131